Once Upon a Farm

A Fairly True Tale

By

Rebecca Horan

For Everatt —
for everything
you've been &
done
R Horan

PublishingWorks, Inc.
Exeter, NH
2009

PublishingWorks, Inc.,
60 Winter Street
Exeter, NH 03833
603-778-9883

For Sales and Orders:
1-800-738-6603 or 603-772-7200

Designed by Anna Pearlman

LCCN: 2009920799
ISBN: 1-933002-94-8
ISBN-13: 978-1-933002-94-1

Printed on recycled paper.

Printed in the United States

Change is Inevitable. Growth is Optional.

In memory of my mother, Cynthia—you always knew I could do it.

ACKNOWLEDGMENTS

This is my first book, though two earlier manuscripts are shivering in the wings like hopeful understudies. It wasn't until my publisher sent back the first edited draft, and I had whined, pouted, resisted the suggested changes, and then finally got over myself and got to work, that I discovered that a book's author is nothing more than a bit player in the finished product! It was a vital lesson for my sensitive ego, and will hopefully make me a better writer.

Now I fully grasp why so many books begin with gratitude and nods to everyone who contributed so significantly to their birth. First there is the labored reading of a partial manuscript, delivered by a desperate neophyte to an acquisitions editor, who spies some kernel of promise, and fertilizes and encourages it so that you don't pitch the whole mess in the woodstove. Thank you, Phil Englehardt. There are the characters (real or created) that you must remain faithful to, or risk doing them a severe injustice. My deep appreciation to all of you, and, of course, a big thanks to the cows. Then there is the practiced, critical eye of a gifted editor, who can praise with one hand and slap you silly with the other. Thank you, Jeremy Townsend—for everything! There are the production and marketing folks, who turn words into visions that enhance the story and give it a fighting chance in the big, wide world. Thank you, Carol, Peg, Kieran, and Anna of PublishingWorks. There are others who have no clue that they even made a contribution, but without their support, love, and encouragement, I wouldn't dare to write at all. Heartfelt thanks to Jay, Liz, Kerry, Everett, and Paul.

Finally, there are the unsung Angels who are always there, whether we acknowledge them or not. Thank you, Christopher Dilts at AskAnAngel.org for introducing us.

CHAPTER ONE

Thursday, July 24th

If there is a lesson here, it is simply this: do *not* drive in the pouring rain. At least not down pleasant, scenic country roads, where you might naturally allow your mind to drift and wander. A fair number of these narrow byways are little more than glorified, paved cart paths and it's important to stay focused on the task at hand, which is to remain within the imaginary (unpainted) sidelines of the tarmac. With the addition of pond-size puddles, a variety of complications can arise. You might not see that small mound of fur skittering across the road, or in the blink of a lazy eye you can be sucked into a steep, treacherous ditch.

If the latter is your misfortune, this is how it goes: After repeated failed attempts to remove your wedged vehicle from its tilted parking spot, a handsome and gallant Prince Charming will not gallop to your rescue. Instead, a grumpy fat guy with a stubby cigar clenched between his last five teeth will eventually arrive in a banged-up tow truck. The logo on his baseball cap is obscured by untold layers of sweat and grease. It must be his busy season, because it's clear he hasn't bathed in several weeks, and his pants have migrated halfway down his stark white bum. If you have a shred of decency, you are forced to look away when he bends to secure the chains. Still, you will feel very small, inept, and stupid as he swears, scratches his crotch, and drags you out. It's usually expensive, and always mortifying.

On this particular morning that's not what happened. But that's how it all started, by driving in the rain on a Thursday morning in July, not really so unlike any other summer morning in New Hampshire, except that it was pouring buckets. Had been for days, weeks it seemed.

I had just picked up my friend and business partner, Liz, and we were silently bouncing cross-country towards Dover, always preferring the quiet, less-traveled roads, sipping coffee and making the occasional murmured comment, requiring no response. Nodding once in a while. It should be noted that I am a morning person, one of those irritating people who gets out bed at 5:00 a.m. ready to launch into conversation. Liz is not, and in the twelve years that we've worked together, I've learned to stifle my impulse to chatter away at her until say, noon—primarily because I love and respect her, and also, it's like talking to a wall. So these mostly silence-observed commutes were a pattern that we'd established during her two month existence without a functional vehicle. But that's another story altogether. Let's stick to this one…

8:25 a.m. – I collect Liz at her house and we start off—we're due in the office by nine o'clock. Having memorized this stretch of lumpy, lonely road, I foolishly allow a wistful daydream of sunnier times. Liz's sudden gasp causes me to slam on the brakes, and I never even see the lone fawn that bolts across the wet road. Almost. I just feel the sickening thud, and his tiny, spotted body skids across the slick black pavement into the aforementioned ditch. Liz and I are transfixed with horror as we kneel beside him. His slender neck is arched back, eyes rolled and fixed, body convulsing in what appears to be the throes of death. There are two pastures on either side of the road, but no sign of a doe.

We cannot leave him to die alone in the rain, to suffer any longer than he must. There is a guilty, grief-laden silence as we begin the transport of the comatose, dying fawn to Broadview Animal Hospital. We glance at one another, but there is nothing to say that will change our part in the vehicular homicide of this innocent creature.

Not far from the hospital, the fawn wakes, screams bloody murder, and morphs into a respectable imitation of Cujo in the back of my Jeep. Liz dives from the front seat, trying to subdue him and prevent further injury, to all of us.

9:05 a.m. – Our arrival at the vet's office is none too soon. We've called ahead to explain our dilemma, and a technician meets us in the parking lot with a blanket. We wrap the panicked fawn securely and rush through the waiting room, carrying our wriggling bundle into the nearest exam room. Cujo slips out of the blanket and promptly tries to kill both of us, the veterinarian, and two technicians. His sharp, flailing hooves make lethally effective weapons. During one scrabbling, upside-down moment, the vet discovers that our fawn is a buck. She is kicked in the head as a reward. We're all battered, bruised, and panting for breath in the struggle to restrain him.

Veterinary evaluation: no broken bones, slight head trauma, possible internal injuries, otherwise fine. Fawn is okay, too.

9:20 a.m. – I call five wildlife rehabilitation centers. No one can or will take our precious, screaming package. I had no idea that deer could make these high-pitched, blood-curdling sounds. Apparently none of the wide-eyed clients in the waiting room did either. We marched past them as they stared, the fawn wrapped tight in the blanket, his frantic squeals muffled slightly.

10:00 a.m. – In the fervent hope that his mother is searching for him, we return the fawn to the pasture where we had our unfortunate interaction. The fawn refuses to leave the roadside and attempts to run back onto the tarmac in front of every passing vehicle. The poor darling is obviously suicidal. We move him further into the pasture, nearer the woods edge, to deter this behavior, inviting new lacerations and bruises. At this point he's beginning to tire, so it's more insult than injury.

We have moved away about a hundred yards where we can observe the fawn, but not disturb the doe if she returns to collect him. The fawn is not moving at all. He bleats occasionally, calling for his mama. Have I mentioned it was raining?

12:30 p.m. – The fawn has not moved and there's no sign of the doe. Still raining.

1:00 p.m. – Another fawn has entered the pasture, about the same size. It meanders around for ten minutes and goes back into woods. Still no sign of the doe, and frankly, I'm a little irritated with her lack of parental responsibility.

1:30 p.m. – Still raining. Harder now.

2:00 p.m. – Swaying, head down, shaking, soaked to the skin, shivering, exhausted. Fawn is doing the same.

2:30 p.m. – In an effort to preserve our own lives, we slip and squish into the Jeep. But we can't bring ourselves to drive away and leave him. It doesn't seem possible, but the weather is deteriorating rapidly and the rain is not falling anymore, but driving sideways.

Just six miles away, though we are unaware of it at the time, our area is having the worst tornado damage it has seen in more than fifty years. One woman is killed, and more than one hundred homes are lost or damaged.

2:45 p.m. – We slog back into the field, pick up the bedraggled, pathetic creature (no longer kicking) and put him in the Jeep, where he immediately curls into a ball and sleeps all the way to my house. On the way, we stop at the grain store and buy a lamb nipple and a small bag of milk replacer. The label says it's suitable for deer.

Fortunately, I'd built a new barn several years before and its equine occupants had departed two years earlier, one to the inevitable afflictions of old age, and the other given to my daughter. I was beginning to think I was nuts paying the rising taxes on my empty property when I really had no intention of filling it up again. Lately I'd even been contemplating selling it.

Liz and I carefully prepared a safe haven for the fawn—a roomy 12' x 12' horse stall bedded with deep pine shavings, a cozy hay pile to curl up in, and a water bucket (in the unlikely event that he has not absorbed enough through his spotted hide). We retreated to the house to put on dry clothes and fix a baby bottle for the fawn. There are no babies in either of our recent pasts, so a twenty-ounce soda bottle and the lamb nipple would have to do.

We lift the sleeping fawn out of the Jeep, carry him to the stall, and do our best to dry him off with a towel. There's no fight left in him and his head is tilted to one side, drooling and gasping for breath. He refuses the bottle, clamping his thin lips tight. By our calculations, he hasn't eaten in at least seven hours and has suffered significant trauma. We force his mouth open, insert the nipple, and gently squeeze the bottle until he finally cooperates by swallowing some of the milk replacer. Then we leave him to rest and trudge back to the house for a much-needed drink ourselves. Liz has a beer and I have a rum, no force necessary. We stare at each other, blank expressions mirrored in our slack, tired faces.

It is 4:00 p.m. and we haven't done a lick of work. We're pretty sure it will be waiting for us in the morning. Liz and I both worked in veterinary medicine for the first ten years of our relationship, and she is a talented large-animal veterinary technician. Two years ago we'd made a simultaneous career change into the mortgage industry, at the precise time that it was failing, of course, but we are determined to make a go of it. Still, none of Liz's expertise with the treatment of sick and injured animals has been forgotten, so our little fawn is in good hands, whether he thinks so or not.

Also on the plus side of this hectic, drenching day, we never had to entertain, or pay, a toothless fat guy.

CHAPTER TWO

Friday

6:00 a.m. – When I rise for the day, it is not without significant moaning and whimpering. I am bruised and sore from knees to nose and swallow a fistful of Aleve so that in another hour, my stiff, middle-aged joints might be persuaded to flex in a feeble imitation of Dorothy's rusted Tin Man. Fix another bottle and shuffle to the barn, fully expecting to find that the fawn has died during the night. He has not. Sleep (for him) is restorative, and he peers up at me from his little nest in the hay. I tiptoe into the stall and slide down the wall to sit beside him. He takes the bottle gratefully, and my aches and pains are forgotten. Or the drugs have kicked in. I walk back to the house and sit on the deck. The sun has risen in the peaceful stillness of a blue, clear sky.

8:00 a.m. – Liz arrives to pick me up. She took the Jeep home last night and reports that she is bruised and aching everywhere. We're in complete agreement with the better-living-through-pharmaceuticals concept. We stare at the fawn for a while and go to work.

4:30 p.m. – The fawn is still alive and the head tilt is not quite so pronounced. He gets up and walks unsteadily around the stall, circling only to the left. He seems to be blind in his left eye, and this adds to his instability. He takes an eight-ounce bottle of milk replacer, his biggest meal yet.

9:00 p.m. – Fawn takes another half bottle, nibbles at some sweet clover that I've picked outside the barn door, and sleeps….

The fawn sleeps, a much needed rest from the trauma of the day and night he's had.

Saturday

5:00 a.m. – Our fawn is much improved, up and trotting around his stall. Takes another bottle, with gusto. I pick a bunch of clover and slice up some apples for him, then run to a neighbor's farm for a bale of fresh-mown, green and tender hay. He is drinking water from a bucket and nibbling at the hay. It appears he will survive.

Noon – He takes another bottle and is looking for the way out. Much too soon. Internet research has helped me to age him as a late-born June fawn, approximately five- or six-weeks-old—far too young to survive without a doe, and I have no interest in feeding the coyotes. I've called a vet friend in Maine who has experience with deer herds, and got the fine details of raising this little fellow to release. I've suspected, and it is confirmed, that I am definitely breaking the law.

In New Hampshire (and most states), it is illegal to possess wildlife of any kind without a permit. Wildlife is the sole property of the State. It seems a rather singular contradiction of terms. I've also learned that if I contact the Fish & Game Department to obtain said permit, they will hastily remove the contraband and either euthanize it or release it. And frankly, though I have no huge authority issue, I'm unwilling to allow either of those outcomes. At least until the little spotted wonder has a fighting chance of making it on his own.

Besides my vet friend, a web site from a ranch in California that has been successfully raising wild black-tail fawns for years is a wealth of information. We will proceed along our clandestine path for at least the next two months. The hopeful plan is that once the fawn has lost his spots and is beyond the nursing stage, the doe and fawn that appear like stealthy shadows in my pasture every evening will allow him to join up with them. It's an admittedly optimistic view, but not impossible.

Earlier in the week (prior to Deer vs. Jeep incident), I'd made plans to take a trip to northern Vermont to see a herd of beefalo cows and their calves. A father and son farming duo in the next town over had purchased six cow/calf pairs during the Vermont farm's herd reduction, and I'd invited myself over to their place to see them. They were magnificent animals—sturdy, strong and virtually indistinguishable from any other beef cow.

Since I was a kid, I'd dreamt of owning cattle, a direct result of spending much of my happy childhood playing with the calves on a nearby dairy, Meredith Farms in Topsfield, Massachusetts. At one point during my high school years, I'd planned on going to college for animal husbandry, and then on to either beef or dairy production. Horses were my first love, then dogs, then cattle. Farming seemed the obvious way to accommodate all of them.

My traditionally suburban mother, who prided herself on a perfectly kept house and tight hospital corners on every bed, had unreasonably strong objections to this plan. First and foremost, no daughter of hers was going to "shovel cow manure for the rest of her life." Mom had her own dreams, one of them being that I might someday outgrow my exaggerated tomboy stage and be magically transformed into a proper lady. And God bless her, she gave it her best shot, but it just wasn't to be. Though I was eventually persuaded to pursue a liberal arts education, abandoning my cattle ranching dream, there was a never ending string of dogs, horses, chickens, even a pig or two, through my adult years. Mom finally resigned herself to my reality, and even came to accept and respect it, particularly when I graced her with her first grandchild. That's when we became friends.

However, even at the advanced age of fifty-three, I'm one of those nut jobs who can be seen standing by the side of the road, hanging over a barb wire fence, admiring the unknown herd in an unknown farmer's field. It's pathetic really, but we are who we are, and in this corporate age of fast-paced technology, I am still a frustrated farmer at heart.

At any rate, with the fawn fed and safely tucked away, I left for Vermont around two o'clock. This is a fairly pleasant drive, particularly on the second nicest summer day in more than a week. I hummed along, enjoying the scenery as I passed through the mountain notches, and looking forward to visiting the farm. Upon arrival nearly three hours later, I decided instantly that I wanted to live there. Particularly if I had to be a cow to do so! Among its many attributes, it is without a doubt located in the most beautiful cattle country I've ever seen in New England. Steep, green hills sweep down to a river valley from the apex of the farm's five hundred acres. Its buildings are neat and handsome in their utilitarian design, and the place is spotless, for a cow farm…

Bob, the farm manager, meets me just inside the barn door. We shake hands and he leads the way to show off his prize Angus cow. She is a stunning black beauty, hefty and solid as a rock. He's justified in his obvious pride, but I didn't come to see Black Angus. I came for the beefalo.

Beefalo are a hybrid of any beef breed and American bison. The desired genetic blend is between 35–38 percent bison, termed "3/8 full-blood." Anything more than this and there are fertility issues, not to mention that they become just a tad difficult to handle. They look like cows, they smell like cows, and for all intents and purposes, they are cows. There are some distinct genetic traits that hint at the bison influence: The ability to utilize grasses and weeds to build protein more efficiently than a regular cow, and there is no need to "finish" them with grain. They grow faster, mature earlier, and can withstand all weather conditions, pretty much without shelter of any kind, though any cow man worth his salt will offer it nonetheless. They are more disease resistant than regular bovine breeds, and they are a little feistier. Not mean, just tougher than cows. Like full-blooded bison, it's not a good idea to get into a staring contest with a beefalo bull, or even a protective new mother. They will charge on occasion, and a three-quarter ton of aggravated, postpartum beef on the hoof is not really ever a brilliant idea—sort of like a possessed Chevy truck with a bad attitude.

Leaving Bob's beautiful Angus behind, we climbed into the farm "mule," a vehicle that suggests another hybrid of a large golf cart and a recreational four-wheeler. It can pretty much go anywhere, and we did, starting with the pasture that contained about twenty-five head of cows with the youngest calves, ranging from two-weeks- to two-months-old. They were bigger than beef calves of the same age, sturdier legs, deeper chests. Not as flighty as regular calves. Gorgeous calves. Beautiful cows. Thick, lush green grass and sparkling clean water tanks. A manager with the herd's best interests at heart, and the pride of excellent bovine management as plain as his broad smile while he talked about them. I tried to ask intelligent questions, but was nearly drunk and delirious with the bounty and beauty of it all. Cow heaven is an actual place in Orleans, Vermont.

After touring the rest of the pastures in the mule, we returned to the barn. While Bob talked about the cows, I noticed a single calf in a steel pipe-pen. It was curled up in the hay, and seemed reasonably content, but alone.

"What's with this little guy?"

"Mother was struck by lightning in the storm on Thursday. He wouldn't steal from the other cows—most of 'em will, but he's just too young. So I been bottle feeding him ever since."

"Really?"

"Ayuh. Not the best timin'. I gotta leave tomorrow for an auction in Maine and it's gonna be a problem."

"What will you do with him?"

He shrugs, declining to answer, but I understand the implication. This lonely, week-old fellow is not long for the world.

"Uh, Bob, how much do you want for that calf?" Plan is hatching as I speak.

He glances sideways to see if I'm serious. "Hundred?"

I wrote a check while he got hold of the hefty orphan, backed the Jeep into the barn, put a half sheet of plywood in between the front seats and the back, and Bob unceremoniously tossed him in. Then he told me how much and how often to feed him (same schedule as the fawn, six times the quantity of milk replacer), and we were down the road. I tried to convince myself that my sole, unselfish motivation was to provide company for the orphan fawn. It was, however, nothing more than a poorly veiled excuse.

The calf bawled his head off for the first half hour, urinated and spewed sloppy poop at the Jeep windows. I opened the sunroof, turned on the air conditioning, and motored homewards. Barreling down the northern highway in the fading light, I was giggling, almost praying that a State Trooper would pull me over. Even a ticket would be worth seeing the look on his face when the calf stuck his head out the back seat window! However, there's never a cop around when you want one. It's a law. Still, I was happy. Content.

Finally, my very own calf!

9:45 p.m. – Home. Calf declines to disembark. First he kicks me, *hard.* Then he butts me with his knobby head when I try to scare him out from the back seat door. It's a stand-off, and we stare at one another with wary distrust and confusion.

10:30 p.m. – I try coaxing him out with a fresh bottle of milk, which he happily slugs down, backing off every time I try to flip a rope over his neck. (In retrospect, the refueling of a vehicle-bound baby with immature multiple stomachs was a bad idea.) He takes a crack at bellowing like a real bull and I laugh at him. Taking both exception to my ridicule and careful aim, he wallops me again.

11:30 p.m. – I give the sweet, gentle fawn another bottle, make one last half-hearted attempt to coax the obstinate calf out of the Jeep. I back into the barn and leave the tailgate open. Then I give up and go to bed. Aggravated. Tired.

Still happy, though.

Sunday

3:00 a.m. – I'm awake because the calf is bawling his damn fool head off. Good, maybe it's jumped out of the Jeep on its own. No such luck.

He is still in there, now ravenously hungry, since he has emptied the entire contents of his digestive system into the Jeep. I realize that if I ever do get the calf out, the Jeep will never be the same. There is not enough industrial-strength detergent in the universe to completely remove calf diarrhea from automobile carpet, and there is no question that I could someday trade it for a newer model. That option has been taken off the table, and I give only passing consideration to putting the calf *on* the table. As soon as I get my hands on him …

Still happy.

4:00 a.m. – Feed the fawn his bottle. Feed the calf (still in Jeep) his bottle. Drink a pot of coffee.

6:00 a.m. – There is no one I know who's up at this hour on a Sunday morning, and who might also be willing to help me haul a big, mad, poop-covered calf out of the Jeep. At least not without collapsing in a fit of uncontrollable hysterics and suggesting that I up my medication. Quite honestly, I'm considering it.

7:00 a.m. – Fawn sleeping. Calf sleeping. Dogs fed, sleeping. I'm hungry and have neglected to do my weekly grocery shopping. One more attempt to remove the calf from his filthy leather and steel pen. Same result, or lack thereof. In the light of day, the Jeep looks pretty bad. I fear that my hundred dollar calf may turn out to be a several thousand dollar new vehicle.

Not quite as happy as before.

7:30 a.m. – Calf on board, I drive to the local diner and order breakfast. I'm too whipped to explain to the regulars there, the familiar faces that I've dined and joked and argued with for twenty years, that I've backed myself into a very tight, smelly corner. I know the jostling and ridicule that will follow, and regardless of how well deserved it may be, I'm just not in the mood.

I might have gotten away with it, but halfway through my eggs, the calf starts mooing pathetically, his pink runny nose poked out the side window.

The full diner empties in twenty seconds, including the cook and waitress, coffee cups and partially consumed meals abandoned for the main attraction parked outside. Things like this don't just show up every day, and I've delivered a treasured opportunity for endless teasing and amused storytelling for the foreseeable future. They'll carry this story home to family members who stayed abed on Sunday morning, to their co-workers and friends, most of whom will think it's exaggerated or even fabricated.

A few folks simply stare, others point and whisper. Most fall down in the dirt parking lot and wet themselves, weakened by their gales of laughter. All agree that it's a fine-looking calf. One especially witty fellow remarks that if it grows up in the Jeep, it will have very short legs. Funny. My previously buoyant mood is beginning to wear thin, and has in fact, soured to outright crankiness, and I'm looking for any likely victim that I can lure back to my place to help me solve the bovine dilemma that is mooing out my manure-streaked windows.

8:30 a.m. – I've found him! You may recall the aforementioned farmer who bought the six cow/calf pairs, and is at least partially responsible for this entire mess in the first place. Well, he has innocently appeared at the diner for the sole purpose of having his breakfast, and is now following me up the ridge towards home. I'm beginning to think of it as a "farm," now that I have actual livestock—

theoretically. Assuming that Tom will have better luck than I did in removing the crusty critter from his four-wheel drive accommodations. And yes, he too became incapacitated with laughter when he opened the back hatch and saw the devastation within. I survived. The calf never even batted his long eyelashes. Eyed Tommy suspiciously. Stamped a foot. Pooped again.

10:00 a.m. – The calf has been successfully extricated from the Jeep. Not without grunting effort (Tom), some impressive swearing (me), and the need for a change of clothes for both of us, but he's out. He is placidly munching sweet clover as Tom admires him.

"It's a thousand dollar bull calf, ya know."

"Uh huh, but I think Bob was all too glad to see him go."

Tom shakes his head, smiling. "You are nuts."

Possibly, but still happy.

CHAPTER THREE

I have decided to name my place "Red Gate Farm," and I can already see the painted gate attached to its lone fence post, beneath the century-old sugar maple that presides over the driveway entrance. It used to be a farm, long before I came here fifteen years ago, and it will be again. Back then most family farms didn't have names—my home was known simply as Harry Gray's place. Harry's brother lived across the dirt road on the other farm, and together they raised chickens, turkeys, and dairy cows. For decades the road itself was called "Harry Gray's Hill," for the simple, sad fact that Farmer Gray met an untimely death after being accidentally gored by the pair of stout oxen that he was moving up the steep road.

In the 1970s a pair of Massachusetts transients bought Harry's place as a weekend getaway, but they had no respect for the history of the Gray family, and no respect at all for the heritage of the land. They cut several of the massive sugar maples for firewood (which is a sin), and then Harry's two hundred-year-old farmhouse burned to the ground in a suspicious fire. After they'd collected the insurance money, they sold the place to my old friend, Chuck Hazelton. Chuck planted at least the same number of maples that had been felled, and built a small post and beam cape from the timbers of an ancient barn he'd dismantled. He cut back the overgrown pasture edges to the rugged stone walls, cleared and brush-hogged and mowed until the fields were restored, and lived there happily until he eventually married his high school sweetheart and moved to Portsmouth. Chuck rented the house out for a few years, and then subdivided the house and four acres away from the larger parcel so I could buy it from him. It was the first and only place that felt like home to me since I was a child.

I've also chosen a name for the calf—Harry. One might assume that it is in honor of this long-dead farmer, and though it's a happy, fitting coincidence, that's not the case at all. It's because on the way home from Vermont, I was fondly recalling my childhood days on the dairy farm and trying to remember the name of the resident champion bull. It eluded me, but at 3:00 a.m., when the Jeep-bound calf woke me, it suddenly returned. *Meredith Harry.*

My fascination with Harry was responsible for the occasional butt warming by the farm herdsman. He had calloused hands the size of pizzas and could dole out a swift swat with stinging authority. In those days it was acceptable for any adult in an even unwilling supervisory position to administer spankings when called for. I used to think Mr. Dunham hated kids and was just plain mean, but now realize that the poor man was probably having a mild coronary as he peeled us off the fence.

Harry lived behind a six-foot-tall steel fence. For obvious reasons, we kids were forbidden to approach Harry, so naturally he became an object of acute, fascinated interest. When the farm hands were distracted, busy with their endless chores, we'd sneak over and climb the pen, entice Harry over with some fresh hay, and give him a pat or two on his thick, white hide. The towering bull seemed to enjoy the attention and rewarded our kindness with sloppy swipes of his gigantic tongue. To be kissed by a 2,000-pound bull is a slippery, drooly affair, but very gratifying. Mr. Dunham failed to see the joy in such moments and only focused on the possibility of us being knocked into the pen at Harry's feet. It proved to us that adults had lost their sense of wonder and adventure.

We also got thumped for riding the yearling heifers in the huge south pasture—strictly forbidden and a crime far more heinous than patting Harry. We might damage their developing udders by cowboying around on them. The man had no sense of humor. And I think by that time he was harboring a secret hope that we might fall into Harry's pen and be stomped to death. It would certainly have made his life easier. It might even have made him smile.

Finally, out of sheer desperation, and in an attempt to bribe us away from our persistent disobedience, he gave us jobs. Every morning we convened at the calf barn and fed the bawling, weaned calves their first bottles of the day. We groomed them and cleaned out their little pens, and let them suck our thumbs until they looked like shriveled prunes. Then we snuck over to see if Harry was near the side of his pipe pen.

So now my own bull calf will sport the name "Red Gate Harry." I like it. It makes me happy. At this stage of my life, finding and treasuring the things that make my heart smile, that make me grateful to be alive, are of primary importance.

The fawn is another matter. Should he even have a name? No, of course not, since he will be released in September to become the biggest, most handsome buck in the thousand-acre forest that surrounds my little corner of the world. It's hard to picture at the moment since he cannot possibly weigh more than twenty-five pounds, but someday he will be a hundred-and-eighty-pound buck that reigns over all the does in this vicinity. I'm sure of it. He will be the star buck of the county. That's it! *Starbuck!*

Calf and fawn meet for the first time.

The fawn and calf are curled up side by side in their stall. Starbuck seems to take great comfort from Harry's presence, and that gives me comfort. Since the beginning, I'd taken pains to avoid patting or cuddling the fawn, which was beyond difficult, particularly when he tried to climb into my lap after his bottle. I had to push him away and leave the stall, and now I'm so glad that I restrained myself. Since Harry's arrival, the fawn comes only close enough to accept the bottle, then moves away, ducking behind his taller friend. I'd much rather the fawn bond to the calf than to a human, since it will increase his chances of survival in the wild. For his part, Harry seems to be quite fond of the little deer and stands over him after their meals, licking his neck and face, which the fawn does not object to. When he's had enough, he politely gets up, moves to another spot, and folds his spindly legs into a delicate, tidy bundle. Harry beds down beside him and they doze for most of the day.

Monday

Starbuck has begun to do an interesting thing. If he becomes irritated or startled, his entire coat stands up on end, making him look like a spotted fluff ball. At first I thought he was cold, but then watched as his coat returned to a sleek, red blanket within seconds. I stamped my foot on the barn floor—poof! Fluff ball.

This morning I've discovered a deer bed just outside the back door of the barn. The long grass is matted in the perfect oval that deer make. There are two spots, one larger than the other. Could this be the doe and fawn of the evening pasture? Perhaps she hears when Starbuck bleats and comes to be near him. It might explain why he is increasingly interested in getting out of the stall. He circles, craning his neck to see the natural daylight over the wall and in the windows. He bleats, circles, puffs up. Then he lies down and sleeps. I'm tempted to release him now, to see if the doe will pick him up, but not sure if she'll let him nurse. And if she doesn't, we're back to the coyote food scenario. Can't do it.

I feed Harry and Starbuck, make sure they have a bucket of fresh water and a pile of sweet hay. Today I've added a bucket of calf starter grain and a mineral-salt block to the stall. They can take it "free choice" if they desire. They are curled up near one another as I leave for work.

Tuesday

The doe has made another bed behind the barn. I'm glad she's coming and certain that Starbuck knows she's there. If this continues up to the time of his release, I feel that my initial plan might work. If she's that interested in him, it weighs the odds in his favor that he'll be invited to join them when he's free. This is very, very cool.

After work I spend two sweaty hours making an outdoor paddock behind the barn. It's fairly simple—four strands of electric wire—and I'm hopeful that the fawn will not try to escape, but my furry toddlers need fresh air and grass. The design of my barn allows them to come and go from the paddock as they please. I'll leave the doors open tonight and hope they're both there in the morning.

Wednesday

It worked! Starbuck and Harry gaze at me from the sawdust bed in their shared stall. The fence is undisturbed and they look content with their new, if relative, freedom. They both take their bottles and settle down for a morning nap. No one is mooing or bleating as I leave for work. Happy.

Liz comes to visit Starbuck late that afternoon and is amazed at his growth over the past seven days. The apparent blindness in his left eye seems to be resolved, and he has been moving normally for a few days. It's been a week and it's hard to believe—it flew by. Summer is officially half-gone and I'm certain that the remaining six weeks will simply evaporate as they always do. But by then it will be time to release Starbuck to his wild deer destiny. I already know that I'll miss the little fellow, but am looking forward to that day of sweet freedom.

But what about Harry? Will he be lonely without his little spotted pal?

CHAPTER FOUR

The answer is that Harry will be anything but lonely. My single orphan calf is about to become part of an unintentional herd. Somehow it just happened, though I clearly acknowledge that these things don't "just happen." Even if subconsciously I engineered it. But I swear it started innocently. Really.

My reminiscences of Meredith Harry, my fond memories of the idyllic days on the Ayrshire farm, has led me on an Internet search to see what became of the farm in particular, and of the breed in general. I discover that Harry, forty years later, is still ranked eighteenth of the top hundred dairy bulls in the country. This is incredibly impressive considering that Harry died four decades ago, and that Ayrshires produce a lesser quantity of milk than other commercial dairy breeds. For an Ayrshire bull to be ranked in the top twenty is a truly remarkable feat.

Since the 50s and 60s, the economic demand for cows to produce as much milk as possible during their ten-month lactation has led to a vastly diminished Ayrshire population. Holsteins have ruled the market since. In the eighteen and early nineteen hundreds, Ayrshire was the most common dairy breed in New England, uniquely suited to the dramatic climate changes and the rugged, rock-strewn hills. Now, not only have the majority of dairy farms disappeared, usurped by sprawling suburban developments and pretty little strip malls, but only devoted small family farms still keep Ayrshires, and there are damn few of those left too.

The determined Internet search led me to a farm in Vermont that is tended by the grandchildren of its original cast. Three adult siblings have followed in their devoted grandparents footsteps, and continue the family legacy of dairy farming with sixty purebred Ayrshires, many of whom are direct descendants of the prolific Meredith Farm bull, or his numerous daughters. To this operation they have added cheese making, creating a unique variety they call "Vermont Ayr." With technology that their ancestors could never have dreamt of, they have marketed this wonderful cheese throughout the northeast and beyond.

I call the farm and ask if it is even remotely possible that they have an extra heifer calf that they'd like to part with. The polite answer, of course, is no. Heifers are the staple of their lives, and this year they've had fewer heifers than bull calves. Would I like a bull calf?

No. I have a bull calf. I want an Ayrshire heifer.

I want one the way a kid wants a new, shiny bike. I nearly vibrate with wanting one. I dream about her grazing in the pasture beside Harry. He is rusty red with a white face. She will be mostly white with red patches strewn about. Her name will be Isabelle. Izzy.

Do I plan to milk her? No, I plan to look at her for the next fifteen years or so. Maybe an errant calf or two along the way, but mostly I want to just see her grazing in the sun. I want to smell her sweet hay breath when I greet her on a winter morning. I want her to be there when Harry is gone, which I don't like to think about now, but there are really only two job descriptions for a beef bull calf: breed or become two years worth of steaks and roasts. I knew this when I brought him home, but choose to ignore that eventual reality. When the time comes, I'll manage. Now he's far too cute and sweet to ponder it.

Isabelle. Where will I find my Isabelle?

In the meantime, Harry and Starbuck are happily mowing the heavy grass behind the barn. I go out to do my final chores of the morning, and as I step to the back door of the barn, I see a doe just beyond the electric fence. She is standing in the deep shade of the crabapple tree, staring at the fawn. She sees me, flicks her tail, but her attention is riveted on the fawn and she doesn't move. Starbuck hasn't seen her yet.

As I watch, she whistles at the fawn. His head shoots up and ears swivel like radar dishes. He walks gingerly towards the fence. A moment passes and I hold my breath. The doe whistles again and Starbuck goes straight up on his hind legs, pops over the four-foot fence as if it were nothing more than a spider web. He stops a couple feet from the doe. She reaches out her delicate, gray muzzle and sniffs him. Then she turns and walks out into the pasture, with Starbuck right behind her. For the briefest fraction of a second my heart leaps into my throat. *No! Too soon.* But nature has its own miracles and tragedies, its own timetable that we far-removed, domesticated humans barely infiltrate.

The doe stops in the middle of the field and drops her head. Another fawn rises out of the long grass and the threesome moves away. I watch until they walk into the woods, and they are gone. In less than a minute, without fanfare or ceremony, Starbuck has vanished.

Now my heart soars. This was the plan all along and the doe beat me to it. September was too long for her to wait, too long for both of them. I offer a silent, fervent prayer that she will protect and teach him. Then I turn back to glance at Harry, concerned that he will be bereft without the fawn. He has already resumed grazing, accepting in a bovine heartbeat that his companion is away.

We could learn a lot from cows.

The final hour—it is the morning of Starbuck's accidental release. He and Harry greet the morning.

CHAPTER FIVE

My bulldog, Tug, is delighted by this new turn of events. He hadn't been allowed in the barn when Starbuck was in residence. Dogs were not something I wanted the fawn to get comfortable with. Now that he's gone, Tug meets Harry for the first time. Tug is not fond of horses, and I watch carefully to make sure he doesn't nip at the calf's nose, but it appears to be love at first sight! They stand for an hour, dreamily licking each other's faces. Harry pulls Tug's ear into his mouth and sucks on it for several minutes, which I'm certain will not be tolerated. But Tug seems to appreciate the sloppy wash down, seems relaxed about the entire thing. Calf and dog have inexplicably bonded, and when I turn to go back to the house, Tug refuses to leave Harry. He lays down on his side of the pipe gate and hangs out with his new best friend for the rest of the day.

Six hours after Starbuck has abandoned the farm, I get a call on my cell phone from a farmer in northern New Hampshire who has heard of my search for an Ayrshire heifer. He has a heifer he explains, but she was twin to a bull calf and therefore called a "freemartin." Due to the exchange of male and female hormones through the shared placenta, it is 90 percent likely that she will be infertile. Would I be interested?

What does she look like, I ask? She is dark red with a small streak of white on her face and splashes of white on her hindquarters. Though she is not the white calf I've dreamt of, it's unlikely that I'll find another this season. When can I come get her? We set the time and like a kid on Christmas Eve, I can hardly wait. The Jeep will have to sustain one more livestock hauling trip. It has become fondly known around town as the "Moo Mobile." It'll be years before I live that one down.

The following afternoon I traipse northward, through roads I haven't traveled in more than twenty years. Blessedly, things have not changed much. There is no metropolitan area within commuting distance, and that fact alone has saved this northern realm from development. In fact, there seem to be even fewer people. As I enter Pike, I note that there are more (quiet) folks in the cemetery than living in the town itself. Once it was a thriving farming town.

But I also notice that there are no more cows. The enormous, valley fields that once supported large dairy herds are now in hay production, or choked with weeds, the deep pine forests encroaching on the edges. Back in the 50s and 60s, New Hampshire was often called "Cow Hampshire" due to it's abundance of dairy cows and relatively miniscule human population. Our family always vacationed in the White Mountain town of North Conway. Back then it was a seasonal hamlet, sleepy even in July. A rushing white-water river ripped through the valley, pine and hemlock scented the thin air, and morning fog rose against the sheer granite cliffs that contained it all.

Today it is mile after mile of high-end factory outlets and congested traffic, impatient consumers in expensive cars racing one another to the next bargain, flinging credit cards with desperate abandon. The river is still there, churning uninterrupted over the glacial deposits of smooth granite boulders, but the air is heavy with automobile exhaust, and the peace shattered by car horns and screeching brakes. I can't go near the place without a heavy, grieving heart.

But back then it was still pristine, and every year I begged Dad to consider moving to the Granite State.

"Honey, no one *lives* in New Hampshire." Because children are astoundingly literal, I thought for the longest time that when winter came, everyone left. But what about the cows, I asked him?

"Well, the farmers live here, of course. But no one else."

Which was precisely the point. It was a life I imagined loving. Placid cows and grass-fattened ponies in green pastures, sparkling lakes, majestic purple mountains, and dark hemlock forests. Heaven. My domestically raised, Massachusetts-born parents were not so easily swayed. It is more than four decades later and I suddenly realize that I am now living the life I dreamt of then. Pause for a prayer of gratitude.

When I arrive at Ferncroft Farm, I'm greeted by Brian and Judy. They are open and friendly, and Brian and I find common ground immediately. He worked at Meredith Farm shortly after he graduated school. We knew the same people there and fondly reminisce before he leads me through the barn to see the calves.

There she is—my new heifer! She is deep mahogany red, with just a few splashes of white on her flanks and legs. Somehow she is not Izzy. But she is Lucille. Lucy in the sky with diamonds!

Lucy has been handled very little in her short seven weeks of life. She's a bit spooky and uncertain, but accepts the calf halter without a great deal of trouble. Me pulling, Brian pushing, we skid her down the barn aisle and onto the wide, green lawn by the house. She has a little bucking fit at the end of the rope and we all chuckle a bit. Brian's glad to have her going to a pet home with someone who will love her. Her infertility makes her useless to him, but it's clear that he and Judy love these cows. The girls in the pasture come to his call, trotting down the grassy hill towards the fence.

Lucy is substantially bigger than Harry, and Brian struggles to lift her into the back of the Jeep. Once in, she scrambles to her feet and looks around with nervous interest. Within thirty seconds she's satisfied that nothing more traumatic will occur and she stands quietly. She only moos for a few minutes as we head back down the hill and turn onto the paved road. By the time I've gone twenty miles, she has lain down and is still and quiet until I get her home. She doesn't poop even once, and had I been a little more on the ball, this might have been my first clue that she and Harry are polar opposites, and that there are no steadfast rules of baby bovine behavior. But I was really caught up in the pleasant, mindless glow of acquiring my second lovely calf.

After an uneventful drive, I parked where Lucy could depart the Jeep by jumping out onto nice, soft grass. Brian has kindly offered me the rope halter that we used to drag her out of the barn (after we'd already removed it, of course), so I'm sure that once I get it on again, the unloading will be much easier than the first calf rodeo.

Good plan, but calves are immune to our best intentions. She was lying down peacefully when I opened the rear hatch, staring at me with what I now recognize as dramatic, feigned innocence. I have only the vaguest recollection of her standing, and then I was lying on the ground as she barreled through me to freedom!

If you will recall, I said that she hadn't been handled much. She trotted away to an adjoining (unfenced) pasture. I called to her, panicky and pleading. She trotted faster. I mooed at her and she stopped. This went on for the next half hour. Trotting, mooing, stopping.

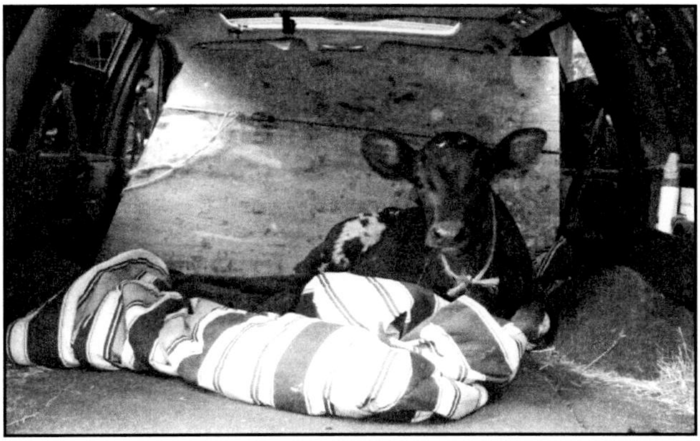

Lucille in the "Moo Mobile" just prior to her bold escape.

Finally I stomped into the barn and retrieved Harry to use as wild calf bait, which seemed a more reasonable (and humane) alternative than the rifle I was eyeing in the corner. I dragged him onto the front lawn with the lead rope that had been intended for the red devil herself. Maybe I could entice her to follow Harry into the barn. No such luck. She'd follow him as far as the driveway, but wouldn't cross it to continue. I tied Harry to a maple tree and went in to make a batch of milk replacer. Harry sucked down the bottle with grunting gusto while Lucy sniffed him all over, but stayed just out of tackling range.

"Luuuccy …" I cooed at her as I inched forward. She looked at me squarely, and I swear there glimmered a dancing flame of crafty intelligence, something decidedly lacking in beef cattle. Then she trotted away jauntily, tail flung over her back. I sat down on the lawn and Harry lay down beside me, resting his milk-soaked chin on my leg, content with a full belly. Lucy grazed. For an hour.

By now it was nearly dusk. Giving up the last hopeful shred of capturing her on my own, I called a distant neighbor. Sue has a nice farm, but no more cattle. She says this is because she grew tired of chasing escaped cows all over hell and back. Sue arrived in short order, and with little fanfare, she pressed Lucy forward as I led Harry into the barn. It took less than three minutes. Farming alone is not always the easiest chore, particularly when you do retarded stuff, like not backing up to the barn door before you open the hatch with a crafty, half-wild calf inside. God bless good neighbors.

Lucy and Harry are fast friends. She's taller than he, almost two months older, and unquestionably smarter, but he's braver and steadier. Though he's not the brightest bulb under anyone's bushel, he's long since figured out that I am the food delivery system.

He powers through the offered bottles while she looks on, refusing to be enticed to come near me. I know that it's only a matter of time before she gives in. In the meantime, she bawls her pretty,

Lucy & Harry graze the overgrown lawn

red head off for three solid days and nights. The cranky neighbors across the road are not impressed and boldly, indignantly inquire what my intentions are with these cows. I'm a little shocked—it's the first time they've spoken to me in ten years. I kindly inform them that under no circumstance will I have more than a hundred.

Perhaps they'll move. Like back to suburbia from whence they came. That would be nice.

CHAPTER SIX

I've flipped the calendar to September, astonished that August is gone. It is four-thirty in the morning and the thermometer hovers at barely forty-eight degrees. The windows are still open and I can see my breath inside the house. Every year I have this little bet with myself, to see if I can hold out till October 1st to turn the heat on. Some falls are more challenging than others. There is a measure of Yankee frugality in this, but it's more a badge of honor among us seasoned northerners. Who can grit their teeth, grab their sweaters, pull on their wool socks, and hold out the longest?

I take my steaming coffee cup out to the deck. A light breeze rustles the treetops and the stars are brilliant in the way that only a dry Canadian cold front can make them. The leaves are just beginning to turn, and the pasture has been grazed down to a respectably trimmed carpet of late summer green. Harry and Lucy spend most of their time together.

In August they were joined by Mae (blonde, buxom, and irreverently pushy) and her red-blonde calf, Isabelle (finally, my "Izzy"). Both of them are beefalo from the Vermont farm, and formerly known as #237 and #237H (heifer). I like my names better. I have no justification for this recent acquisition, and since I'm the only one paying the mortgage and associated bills, I don't feel that one is necessary. If pressed for an answer, I'd have to say that it just makes me happy. But I promise myself that this is the extent of my small herd, at least for the moment.

It's likely that Mae is already in calf to the red bull that shared their pasture in Vermont. However, Harry is due to be castrated next month and is destined for the freezer in another year. If Mae calves next spring, they will be briefly five, then four again. Lucy will never have babies, and Izzy is a couple years away from the possibility of motherhood. I have only ten acres of grass available, which includes borrowing the use of Chuck's back field. It's enough to comfortably support four or five fat bovines, but no more. At least that's what I tell myself.

Mae and Izzy in their new home. It is now an official herd.

The night that Mae got off the livestock trailer and ambled into a stall, with Izzy nearly tucked up her bum in the rush to avoid human contact, Lucy reacted like Santa Claus had just delivered her heart's desire. She bawled and threw herself at the stall door until morning when I let the newcomers out into the pasture. Mae had just cleared the barn doors when Lucy launched her red baby body at the huge cow. Mae backed up, lowered her head and stomped her foot in an effort to discourage her, but Lucy wasn't paying attention. She had been weaned from her own mother the day I'd picked her up, so unlike Harry, she knew precisely what cows were for, and the only thing on her mind was Mae's swollen udder.

Mae had other ideas, and sharing her calf's milk with an odd-looking, whirling dervish dairy creature wasn't one of them. But Lucy was single-minded in her pursuit. For days she plagued Mae with constant demands, circling her, ducking in for quick sips, sneaking in between her hind legs. Mae was not above giving her the boot, or lifting Lucy's small red body with her massive head and tossing her a good ten feet. But Lucy was undeterred. Harry stayed out of the fray and watched with complete incomprehension. He had no recollection of cow udders and trotted to me for his bottle, spinning around my knees frantically if I didn't give it to him fast enough.

At the end of a week, Mae had finally given in, and now she had two calves, one she loved and protected, one she barely tolerated, and thrown in for good measure, a third who used her only for shelter and shade. Now that she was feeding two growing calves, I upped her grain ration and made sure the hundred-gallon water tank was always clean and full. It was astonishing the quantity of water she could consume in one hot summer day.

I was guzzling down my own share of cold well water, nearly a gallon a day, which I sweat out just as quickly. In the month since Starbuck and the calves arrived, I've done more outside chores and projects than I have accomplished in the last five years. I'm not sure exactly why, but in some fashion they motivate me to put time and energy into the place. One day I found myself redecorating the interior of the barn. At first I wasn't aware of doing it, just straightening up, moving things from place to place, reorganizing. Then I was hanging strings of Christmas lights up along the top of the walls, painting a little side table, setting up a comfortable camp chair and plopping an extra dog bed down next to it. I stopped short of putting a candle on the table, and only because of the potential fire hazard, but I ate dinner that night sitting in the barn doorway. The late summer breeze delivered the vanilla scent of lilies, and because it's what I imagine they would prefer, the radio is playing soft country music. Tug curled into his bed, resting his chin on the cool concrete floor, gazing at Harry. I watched the calves as they chewed their cud, and they watched me. In deference to their bovine sensibilities, I ate fish.

I'd safely bet that the television hasn't been on more than a couple hours in the last five weeks. That's a good thing as it's a complete waste of time and attention, a mindless habit that we all fall prey to, particularly in the long, dark winter months. I decide that I will take the last available stall and turn it into a workshop. I'm not quite certain what I'm going to actually produce in the shop, but am confident that it will come to me. I might even put a little woodstove out there so I can avoid the television-winter syndrome. The cows will appreciate the warmth during a snowstorm.

This is when I begin to question what's happening to me. The better part of the last decade had been a series of one misadventure and calamity after another, and in the thick of it I'd been attacked by a lengthy, debilitating depression. Life itself became a precarious tight rope walk, and the desire to put myself to any task was completely non-existent. Opening my eyes in the morning was hard enough. I worked simply because I didn't want to lose the house slightly more than I didn't want to get out of bed. And not because I was overly attached to it anymore, but the thought of moving due to my own abject failure seemed a Herculean, shameful task. That lasted for two years. Maybe more.

But this summer something happened. I noticed one day that I was looking forward to my work, my time with friends (who were very forgiving of my lengthy absence), and to getting home at the end of the day. I planted flowers and freshened the paint on the outside doors. Several months before, I'd started a disciplined practice of daily gratitude, listing all the things I was grateful for every morning and every night, and it had lifted me over the lip of my dull, flattened mood. Was this the reward? Had I created it or had the Universe delivered it?

Then Starbuck appeared in front of me that late July morning. Then Harry and Lucy. Then Mae and Izzy. I find that I am enjoying the whole of my life in a way I haven't for years. And I'm appreciating all of it, every thing that presents itself for consideration. I'm saying "yes" again, and I'm remembering to say thank you. To … well, to something. To the Universe, or God, or whomever is responsible for all of this, because it is quite obviously beyond the scope of human industry. I'm rebuilding the tornado-damaged structure, creating meaning and purpose as I go, inch by inch, day by day. I thought that purpose had to be grand and important. That was my inherent mistake, and for long months I agonized over what I was *supposed* to be doing. Though I searched and prayed and pleaded, nothing came to me. Finally I quit asking, and then the cows arrived.

I know it sounds silly, and that's okay. But I love these cows, and with the same childlike joy that I loved the cows at Meredith Farm. I'm fishing again, laughing with anyone that will pause to enjoy it, investing in my home, creating the farm I always dreamt of, making plans to travel this winter to my favorite place in the Caribbean.

A year ago, I could not have imagined that the pendulum would swing back this way. In fact, what I did imagine is that I would never be happy or lighthearted again. I would just go through the motions—breathe in, breathe out, until my hourglass ran down.

To be fair and impartial, this may have been due to hormonal changes, at least in part. Menopause and its accompanying little "disturbances" seem to have mostly passed. Geez Louise, it's about damn time! For me, it's been a long haul, and I sympathize with any woman going through it. And I apologize to any poor unfortunate in my rampaging, confused path during those years. In my youth, I foolishly thought that I'd sail through these life changes with nary a twitch. If one can survive a loveless early marriage, the inevitable divorce, single-parent child rearing, the deaths of many loved ones, can't one be reasonably expected to withstand the occasional hormonal swing with good grace, kindness, and patience? Apparently not.

But, there you have it—another one of life's little surprises.

And what did I learn through all of it? Mostly this: We tend to take ourselves too seriously; we tend to focus on insignificant details, turning a blind eye to the bigger picture. It's like a great painting by a master. Brush strokes are brilliant, the colors vibrant, or soft and alluring. But if we stand across the room, rather than nose to canvas, we begin to see the entirety, the perfect flow and creation, and if we contemplate it long enough, the subtly insistent message behind the oil veneer.

That's what life feels like now—a partially completed masterpiece that somewhere along its creative way took on its own life force and direction. There is the subject of the painting (somewhat off center, of course), and then there is the unseen master, filling in the spaces, breathing life into its stillness, bringing all of it to motion and living color.

CHAPTER SEVEN

I haven't mentioned Jack yet. No, he is not another homeless, wayward cow. Jack is Liz's cousin, as well as one of her most treasured friends. Jack is a hell of a guy—outgoing, adventurous, a true woodsman. And Jack is dying. I know, I know—we're all dying. But Jack is dying sooner rather than later. Several years ago he was diagnosed with a terminal disease: systemic scleroderma. Never heard of it? You're not alone. No one who has not been directly impacted by this particular monster has heard of it. It's a relatively rare auto-immune disease, for the most part untreatable and in the most severe form, always fatal.

Jack is forty-two years old, and except for the fact that he will die soon, he is the picture of fitness and health. His disease process is almost invisible to everyone else. So far he's gotten away without telling all but the closest people in his life. This does not include his parents, from whom Jack has been estranged for many years. If they ran into him on the street, they would not know that their son is dying. They might think (if they spoke to him at all) that he was just recovering from double pneumonia. His lungs are failing and he coughs harshly when he exerts himself, or laughs heartily, as he is still prone to do.

Jack might be able to survive a few extra years if he could get a lung transplant, but all efforts to accomplish this have fallen short. He can't even get an appointment with the specialist who deals with lung transplants in scleroderma patients. This is a brutal disease—it moves with savage relentlessness, far more quickly than the boggy medical system can cope with.

Anyway, Jack has fully accepted that his days are numbered. The rest of us are having some trouble with it. In the meantime, though he can barely get out of bed on the worst days, Jack continues to pursue life. He goes to work when he can, and he takes his beloved dogs out for hikes when his lungs allow. Unmarried and childless, Jack worries about the dogs, about who will take them and give them a good quality of life and plenty of love when he is gone. In the five years of these dogs' lives, they have rarely spent a day or night away from Jack. It doesn't need to be said, but our pets should not outlive us.

Some of his days are better than others. Some of them just plain suck.

Jack lives in a little rented house that is heated entirely by wood, and last winter was a real struggle for him. None of us are sure how he managed it. It's clear that this summer will be his last living alone, and he is a fiercely independent man.

Five years ago I'd built an addition on my small house, intended as an apartment for my best friend, Sally. There were other factors, lingering issues that we had successfully ignored or avoided for years, but our close living arrangement finally strained our twenty-year relationship to the breaking point. She lived there for two tension-filled years and moved out two summers ago, a hailstorm of angry words and shredded hearts trailing in her turbulent wake. It was smack in the midst of my career-ending depression, of course, and I mourned her loss deeply and for far too long. My adult daughter came home briefly between job and boyfriend changes, but it's about to be empty again.

Liz and I have been trying to convince Jack that it would be a good place for him to live. He can have his privacy, even his own entrance, come and go as he pleases. There is a large fenced yard that the dogs will enjoy, and I'll be around if Jack needs help. Also, it is not heated with wood and I'm accustomed to shoveling the decks and walks, so the physical burden of those chores will be lifted from him.

Finally, he reluctantly agrees. He will move in at the beginning of October. I know all too well what he's struggling with—needing help, resenting the need, resisting it. But Jack is not a stupid man and he knows when to say when.

I hope he likes cows.

My beefalo farmer friend, Tommy, likes cows. Tommy seems to like me, and it's fairly certain that I like him. His company is soothing, strong, and steady, which is the tiniest bit unsettling for any number of reasons. First of all, I've been aware of Tom's existence for at least twenty years, but we had only a nodding acquaintance. He wasn't always like this—far from it, in fact. In his younger, wilder days he was a hard-driving guy who had a tendency towards belligerence when he drank, which was often, and almost always too much. Back then I considered him one of the best looking men I'd ever seen, but his unpredictable, explosive behavior intimidated me. I'm not a sissy or easily frightened, but something about the raw, reckless power of Tom's intensity spelled trouble, and I steered well clear of him. Not to mention that he was married. I'm not sure what happened, but in the years since I'd last seen him, something dramatic has changed. For one thing, the wife is history. I don't ask. It's his business.

But I would like to ask him where that other guy went, and who this new and improved version is. I'm not sure this apparent transformation can be trusted, or if it's simply a new skill he's learned, a clever cover for his true identity. However, I tend to trust my gut instincts when I look into someone's eyes, believing that they are indeed, windows to the soul. And now Tom's clear eyes are vibrantly blue and quick, expressing nothing more than humor and good nature. Also, there's something approaching a peaceful sense of joy and contentment. He reminds me of someone from my childhood, but I can't put a name to it. It's both comfortable and stimulating to be with Tom. He makes me laugh, and he gently reminds me that God's hand is in all of it.

Ah, that's it then! I sincerely doubt that Tom and the Almighty were on an intimate, first-name basis in the old days. But then, neither was I. I'm still not, because frankly, what could God possibly have to say to me? Except maybe "Hey, you there, what's with all the cows?"

Over the bulk of my adult life, I've had no interest in religion. I've found my peace and prayers in nature. I have recently shown a growing interest in spiritual explorations, mostly around meditation, reincarnation, spirit guides, and angels. God is just too big to contemplate. I prefer to take smaller bites.

In the last few years though, I've taken to calling God "Universe"—in my mind that word is so enormous, immeasurable, and so clearly all-encompassing that it more accurately describes my concept and feel of Him. Tom keeps it simple. *God.* His easy acceptance of that name is all-encompassing too.

Tommy drove to Vermont with me, dragging a borrowed stock trailer to pick up Mae and Izzy (an adult cow was not going to be squeezed into the Moo Mobile). This was clearly not his responsibility, simply an act of generosity. We drove north through country we both loved, noting that the uppermost leaves of the hardwoods were beginning their seasonal change. In farmers this creates an immediate sense of urgency. There is the last hay crop to get in, piles of firewood to be split and stacked, garden crops to harvest, and fences to mend. These necessary chores must be accomplished before first snow flies. When the thermometer tops eighty degrees, sweat is rolling down your back, soaking your underwear, and you'd rather plunge into a cold lake, the farm and the animals always come first.

Tom understands this, accepts it without complaint, and I think he likes that I understand it too. We talk about going fishing in the fall, but it's unlikely it will really happen. Time in the fall is borrowed, every day a hustled reprieve from the approaching winter.

These distracting, pleasant thoughts about Tom carry a vague discomfort for me. I've been alone a long time, by choice. It's been six years since my last romantic relationship, and it's been more than fifteen years since I last lived with a man, twenty-five years since I'd abandoned my early, misbegotten marriage. After that, relationships were hard for me. I had a child to raise and she always came first, though I have a feeling she might disagree.

It was hard to find the right man to fit in to that scenario, and to be perfectly honest, it wasn't always them that didn't fit. Most of the time, it was me. There was something unsettled in me that chafed against the constriction of a truly committed relationship. I was used to providing for myself, and used to handling every bit of the responsibility. At the time, I complained that the man of the moment didn't step up to help. Now I can clearly see that I crowded the plate, didn't leave room for them to even take an honest swing.

I noticed it again on the trip to Vermont with Tom. I moved to do the things that were his to do with the truck and trailer. He graciously and firmly did them himself, appreciating the helping hand I offered. But it wasn't necessary, and that was clear. Along the highway, at 65 mph, we blew a tire on the truck. Tom adeptly kept the trailer straight until we'd stopped in the breakdown lane. Never flinched or swore. Pulled out the spare and the jack, and had us on the road again in less than fifteen minutes. I stood there feeling utterly useless, and in strong, capable hands. Comfortable. Safe. Hmmm.

From one northbound state to another and back again, Tom and I discovered that this new spirituality that we'd each been moving towards is a personal necessity and a shared passion. He's far more pure in his pursuit. I use books to find my path, and I try to reason and think my way through it, which is really pretty amusing when I pause long enough to examine it. I'm trying to *think* my way through a spiritual quest!

Tom uses only one book, his heart, and his church.

Among the many other things that I've never been, or even dreamt of being (beauty queen, elegant dancer, fabulous athlete, snazzy dresser, graceful, diplomatic, patient—I could go on), I have never been a joiner. I hated Girl Scouts, not to mention those hideous green uniforms! In high school I never joined a single club, academic, artistic, literary, or otherwise. Nor have I been tempted even once to acquire a gym membership, or join even so much as a book club. So I am not a bona fide member of the non-denominational church that I try to get to once a month. I'm a drop-in, always welcomed with open arms, but just a visitor. I take what I need, and I go. This particular church is too far away for convenience, and the current soaring price of gasoline is another significant deterrent. These are the excuses I use.

The truth is that with a great-grandfather as a fundamentalist Baptist minister, living and preaching into his centennial years, organized religion is not something I'm drawn to, not something that I *think* I need to feel God's presence. I feel it inside. Then I forget, of course, and I have to find my way back in a lurching, sideways gait, only to arrive at the starting line once again. It's anything but a straight, smooth course. It's been more of a roller coaster ride, careening around the sharp corners of my mind, straining and clacking up the steep inclines of anxiety, plunging with hair-raising velocity into the abyss of recurrent depression.

A psychiatrist I consulted once, for the sole purpose of obtaining some pharmaceutical relief, told me I was having a "crisis of ascension." He didn't bother explaining precisely what that was, whether it was a good thing or a bad thing, and I was frankly only concerned with his prescription pad, so I didn't bother asking.

Occasionally (okay, almost daily) I struggle with the question of why I should embark (or continue) on this spiritual journey at all—it's downright exhausting sometimes. Then without warning, a startling moment of crystal clarity, transcendence even, sweeps in to overwhelm and astound me. It quiets my busy, chattering brain, transforms it to the stillness of a reflecting pool. I am filled with a deep, calm certainty that everything is as it should be. I think.

For Tommy, it's truly serious and firmly rooted where it belongs—in his heart. This does not make him a dull, pious boy. He has integrated and balanced it nicely with all the energy and humor of his old self, keeping the best parts of his big personality intact, tossing out the bits and pieces that didn't serve him. I'm envious of his devotion, intrigued by the simplicity of his acceptance. And if I could just ask the Almighty to step aside for a moment, I'd openly admit that I couldn't help wondering that particular night, after he'd delivered my cows safely to their new home and given me a quick, tired hug in parting, whether he's adopted the entire retinue of sin. There wasn't any apparent sin when he'd lifted his t-shirt to show me the tattoo of a raging bull on his smooth, tan chest. I wanted to touch it—not the tattoo, just his warm skin—but stopped myself in the slimmest breath of time. During a general discussion of money, Tom casually mentioned that it was a sin to gamble. Of course, that's a given.

But is it still a sin to covet your neighbor, to make love with someone who is not your spouse, even if you are without a spouse, as we both are? I, for one, can not buy this. Making love with unselfish pleasure and the desire to bring to each other an intimate connection, without any intention of taking what is not yours to enjoy, cannot possibly be a sin. Can it? To me it's nothing short of a celebration—of Life, of God and His creations. But I don't know if Tommy sees it that way, and I'm not sure that I want to marry him to find out. I am, however, becoming more certain that I'd like to ask. Someday. When my tongue gets untwisted and can form the question without the impending danger of puking all over his shoes.

I remember my practice of gratitude right before I fall asleep that night. "Thank you for this wonderful day. I'm so grateful for Tom's generosity and kindness."

I don't say it out loud, but I'm overflowing with gratitude to have spent the whole day in the company of a handsome, capable, smiling man, whose eyes twinkle as he speaks.

CHAPTER EIGHT

Jack is moving in on Saturday. It is not a gigantic undertaking as he has little more than his clothes, tools, and dogs. Liz and I have scrounged up adequate furniture to fill in the blank spaces, and a large, comfortable bed that he and the dogs can share. I expect my spoiled, selfish dog will have his nose out of joint for a couple days, but it won't kill him. It might even make him a better dog. Liz scoffs and snorts at this. Tug is not her favorite canine character, and she's skeptical that he has the ability or desire to evolve.

On Sunday I'm going to church with Tommy, which will serve no less than three purposes. Firstly, if I like it then my arbitrary church-going commute will be shortened from eighty minutes to twenty minutes—big plus. Secondly, it will give Jack some quiet time to settle in, and get to know his surroundings without me chattering away at him, which I would do despite myself. It's the good hostess thing—can't break myself of it.

And lastly, even though I might be the only one who thinks so, it will also be my second unofficial date with Tom. I *know*, unless you are Mormon or Quaker, church should not be considered a date. That is most assuredly not its primary function. Neither is cattle transportation, but my runaway feelings are what they are. I'm trying to rein them in, but they have an extraordinary will of their own, a stampeding-herd mentality.

So I'm looking forward to this service in a rather unique, unholy fashion. I know there will be at least one solid hour that I sit in a pew beside Tom. If I'm lucky and God smiles on me, at some point the minister will ask everyone to join hands. I know, I know, it's on the pathetic, juvenile side of ridiculous. But really, who could blame me? If you'd looked into those bright blue eyes while he was smiling or teasing, and if you'd felt the solid, steady comfort of him, you'd understand.

What I'm really trying *not* to do is get way ahead of myself, set myself up for serious, heart-breaking disappointment. But it's singularly difficult. Because while I'm fully capable of facing the fact that Tom may not now (or ever) have the same budding feelings towards me, I'm enjoying the sheer pleasure of my indulgent little fantasy. I probably won't enjoy it if that's all it ever is, and I might even learn to regret these feelings, but I don't think so.

Since opening my heart and soul again, I can't seem to truly regret anything that comes up. Even when I slip and get angry or frustrated, I try to see it as reminder for the future. I'm being a lot more gentle with myself, a lot less critical than I used to be. And what's particularly interesting is that since I have begun treating myself with higher regard, so are other people. Cool how that works. Sort of a shame that it took me half a century to figure it out, but better late than never, I guess.

At the moment, I feel like a teenager with a first crush. Not quite so over the top and impatient as three and a half decades ago, but excited and squirrely all the same. When I think of him, I feel a lovely rush of tingling warmth in my chest. It could be indigestion, I guess. But is it possible that this is the shriveled romance chamber of my heart? Well, it could certainly use a jump start. When I don't talk to him or see him for too many days in a row, I miss him. That actually freaks me out a little, so I try not to think of him too often. It doesn't usually work out though. Now that it's had a little exercise, my heart seems to have a mind of its own.

This all comes as a bit of a surprise, because I've been purposely alone and disinterested for so long. I was fully prepared to travel the rest of this life path on my own, really had not even considered the possibility of another relationship in my swiftly graying, wrinkling future. And maybe that's what this is—a harmless crush, a practice run for what comes next. Or even what doesn't.

I escape the twirl of my confused ruminations about all this "boy stuff" with the routine of farm chores. In the chilly fall nights, the cows have started sleeping (and pooping) in the barn. In one short night the four of them can manufacture enough mushy cow flaps to fill two wheelbarrows to overflowing. I'm not sure how it's possible, but they seem to produce more waste than they ingest in raw materials.

Between them, they drink almost a full tank of water in a twenty-four-hour period. So every day I scrub it clean, rinse it, and fill it back up for them. They hear the hose running and come ambling up from the pasture to watch the process in a circle around me. On hot days I hold my thumb over the end and direct the spray straight up so that it rains down on their backs. They seem to enjoy this immensely. Once the tank is full, Mae is the first to drink, then the calves one by one. They drain half of it before they wander off, so I fill it again.

Then there is the constant maintenance of the fence line. Someone is always trying to squeeze through or crawl under somewhere, because the grass on the other side is at least a quarter-inch taller, or one shade greener, or simply because the mere existence of a fence demands testing. At least once a week I fill a bucket with fence tools and wire, and make the hilly trek to check every foot of fence. And I'm never disappointed; there is always something to fix—a broken wire here, a snapped insulator, a tree branch that's fallen across the line, or a rock that rolled off the stone wall and lays against the bottom wire, interrupting the circuit. It's hot, sweaty work and somehow I usually end up bleeding. Lifting that last rock made me long for a tractor, or an able-bodied man, and that had my brain skittering back to Tom.

Maybe Tommy isn't the one, the partner that I could possibly share the last third of my life with, though at the moment that is my hidden, secret desire. But if nothing else, maybe he is the gateway to the open question of a partnership. Please note that I did not say *marriage*. I don't really care about that. If that's where things with Tom, or another man, naturally lead, then that would be alright. I guess. I'm not dead set against it or anything, but the institution of marriage isn't a prerequisite or a guarantee of happiness, or commitment for that matter. I've divested myself of that myth a long time ago. And I know lots of people who are devoted, committed partners without benefit of a legally binding marriage certificate. Not so many happy, devoted couples who are married. At least not for any significant length of time.

The first church service is all that I expected and more, except for the noticeable absence of hand holding. I wish there were comment cards so I could suggest this as a pleasant new tradition. Despite this minor irritation, the minister is dynamic in his presentation and manner, gentle in his heart. I like him a lot, and the congregation seems to adore and respect him. This makes a happy, peaceful church.

Tom is focused and attentive to the service. I'm a little more on the tingly, edgy side, sitting next to him and feeling the static electricity that jumps between our resting arms, not touching, but close enough to feel the heat of him. He listens intently and nods on occasion, responds when called to. He is fully engaged in the interactive process of this church. When I clear my throat after a hymn, he quietly hands me a peppermint. Sweet.

I try to listen closely, but there's another voice in my head, something more insistent that's whispering in my ear. *Touch him.* But I don't. Church really is not the appropriate venue for physical gestures of a romantic nature. Compassion, caring, concern, fellowship—yes. Not so much the kind of touch that makes your stomach twist and tighten.

Despite the distraction, I get a lot out of the service. The social gathering afterwards is warm and pleasant, too. Tom has made it his sole responsibility to introduce me to nearly every member of the congregation, so there's no shortage of folks to talk to. I watch Tom across the room as he visits with his fellow parishioners. His wide, easy smile is genuine, and his eyes light up the same for each person he engages. Every once in a while he glances over to check on me, to see if I'm standing alone and need attention. I'm not and I don't. He grins, winks, and goes back to his conversation.

If there is a downside, it's my own doing. I

discover that these congregants dress for church, in the way we did when we were young. The men wear suits and ties. The ladies wear dresses. I really hope that I've not embarrassed Tommy by wearing casual slacks and a summer blouse. And it's clear that if I intend to go again, I'm going to have to purchase a dress. And shoes. No big deal, except that I haven't worn a dress in at least two decades, and I've been ridiculously stubborn about it, avoiding any gatherings in which a dress might be a requirement. Hey, I never said that I'm without my own lingering issues! But he just might be worth it.

On the ride back to his farm where I've left my car, Tom turns to me. "What did you think?"

His eyes twinkle, but he's a little concerned, a little protective of his church. He wonders if I'll criticize it. Silly man. But we all have our insecurities, particularly when something is so vitally important to us and we've brought a stranger into the circle. I recognize that he cares what my opinion is. That's a good sign.

"I liked it, Tommy. It's a very nice group of people, open and welcoming, and the minister is really good."

He nods and the relief that shows in the relaxed line of his jaw allows him to turn back to the road. "Would you like to go again?"

"Absolutely. Especially if I get to go with you." I laugh lightly and he grins a little, enjoying the innocent flirtation. Poor man. If he only knew.

"But of course." A few seconds later, "... Next Sunday?"

"Sure." I try to keep my eyes focused on the road.

It's a thin strand that connects us, but it's enough for the moment. My heart is skipping beats and my palms are sweaty. I want to reach over and take his hand, but something wiser than I can rightfully claim whispers that he's the sort of man who would rather be the one to make this happen. But not yet. It isn't here yet, and I remind myself that there truly is a time for everything, just not always on our own demented schedule. Tom will be, if nothing else, an opportunity to practice patience. I've never been patient. I have been the antithesis of patient. I guess I'm about to learn, and ready or not, I have the distinct feeling that this is precisely the time allotted for it.

CHAPTER NINE

On the Saturday before our second church outing, we had a leftover cattle chore to do. Tom had succumbed to the lure of "just one more" when we were in Vermont. The borrowed trailer that had ferried our cows to their respective homes had been dropped at the mechanic's for an inspection sticker, which might have been a prudent thought prior to our excursion. The state trooper who stopped to check on us during the tire change had been kind enough to point out this oversight, kinder still to refrain from issuing a ticket. Now it was inspected and completely legal for it's short trip home to my generous neighbor. Lisa could have gone after the trailer herself, but Tom insisted that we would do this for her. We decided to go to breakfast, pick up grain at the feed store, then collect the trailer and drag it back to her house.

We met on the corner at the bottom of my ridge, and I jumped into the truck. Off we went down the open road, chatting away like old pals. When we had taken our seats in the diner booth, ordered breakfast and it had been delivered to the table, I noticed that Tommy had gone suddenly quiet and was squirming around a bit.

"Do you want to say Grace, Tom?"

His eyes widened. "You read my mind! How did you know?"

I shrugged and he grinned before bowing his head and saying a beautiful, ad lib prayer of thanksgiving. Nothing rote for this man—just shoot from the hip, or the heart as the case may be. He asked God to help make the day go well, and he thanked Him for my company. No embarrassment or hesitation at all. My heart smiled. And we ate.

We had just finished our meal when we began telling each other stories about our spoiled rotten cows and how they had come to expect their morning ration of grain, loudly demanding it the moment they saw any signs of life, pre-dawn or not. Mae, I told him, bellowed like she was in imminent, life-threatening danger, and I had taken to sneaking around in the dark inside my own house, afraid to turn on a light. This in deference to my grumpy neighbors, who despite my dislike of them, have every right to expect to sleep past 5:00 a.m. without being forced to their elderly feet by an obnoxious, demented cow. She's a very big cow, and she puts all of her sixteen hundred pounds behind her voice. If she were vertical and appropriately attired, she would be an opera diva.

Tommy was having the same difficulties with his herd, and since he rents three apartments in one of the renovated barns, he feels terrible if they wake his tenants. So like me, he finds himself ducking behind out buildings, sprinting towards hulking farm equipment in the dark, trying to avoid radar detection by the on-duty bovine squad. For whatever reason, the recounting of these silly tales sent us into uncontrolled, screaming fits of hysteria. And the harder we tried to stop, the more we laughed, until tears ran down his cheeks and I got a case of the hiccups.

"We could just stop graining them," I suggested.

"No, I don't think we can. I couldn't take three solid days of that bellowing." More wailing laughter ensues until we are weakened and helpless.

"We have to go," he croaked, lurching to his feet. The other diners were beginning to get aggravated, and the waitress was now giggling along with us, though she had no idea why.

"Tom ..."

"No, please," he wailed. "Don't look at me or talk to me until we get outside." He threw money at the waitress and fled. I followed along, still laughing, and we got into the truck and continued our day. Three times in less than an hour we missed the turns for the well-known stops we were supposed to make. Too busy entertaining one another, lost in conversation and communion. I hadn't enjoyed a day with anyone so much in years, and all we were doing was farm chores. Tom's eyes crinkled when he smiled, which was constant. He grinned and chuckled, made silly jokes and laughed at mine. We dropped the trailer off and he took me home to deliver my load of grain. Then we headed back down the mountain so I could pick up my Jeep at the bottom. It was hard to say goodbye, but the joy we had brought each other stayed with me the entire day. I laughed often just remembering.

The next morning we sat beside each other in church, listening to the pastor, singing hymns and pretending that everything was completely normal. We purposely avoided eye contact, just in case the giggles weren't completely gone, but it wasn't lost or forgotten. What's getting harder every day to recall is the man Tommy used to be.

Mornings on my little farm are my favorite part of the day. I rise between four-thirty and five o'clock, tiptoe down to make a cup of coffee and write in the dark for an hour or two. Then I carry a second steaming cup out to the deck and watch the sunrise over the pasture. As the light reaches into the dim corners near the woods, the cows rock to their feet and begin to graze. Except for this morning. This morning they are nowhere to be seen, or heard. Mae's familiar bellow doesn't ring off the walls, and Harry doesn't moo for his bottle. They are gone—all of them!

Wearing old, tattered pajamas, I jump into the Jeep and begin the hunt for them. My home is surrounded by thousands of acres of blueberry pastures and mature forest. They could be anywhere. By eight I've checked in with all the neighbors in a two-mile radius. No one has seen hide nor hair of them. I finally have to give up the search and go to work.

At two o'clock I'm back on the ridge again, traipsing through the narrow woods trails with a bucket of grain, calling Mae's name, which she does know, but doesn't respond to. Seriously, how does one hide a three-quarter-ton cow? Finally, two hours later, I find a nice fresh cow pie in the highest blueberry field, about a mile from home. Still no cows, but at least I know they've passed this way. I hope that Harry has remembered to follow Mae and the others—he's sweet, but dumb as a rock and has been known to lose them in the tall grass of his home pasture. Suddenly I'm worried about coyotes again. If Harry becomes separated, a pack of them could easily take him down.

Because livestock always chooses the most inopportune moments to pull these amusing little escapades, the pastor and his wife are due at my house for a complimentary social visit at four-thirty. I race home to wait for them. When they arrive, I explain the situation and enlist their gracious help. We drive and search and call, and the pastor and I hike through a few more wooded trails that connect the blueberry fields. Still nothing. By nine o'clock I've walked many fruitless miles and drop into bed exhausted. My sole accomplishment for the day is not swearing a blue streak in front of my pious guests.

In the dim light of pre-dawn, I wake to a distant cow bellow. Mae! I yank my muddy boots on and head out the door, back to the place where I found a sign of them the previous morning. As I drive over the washed-out rubble of the dirt trail, round the last bend into the high pasture, there they are. Mae is grazing and the calves are wandering around in confused circles. Harry trots toward me as I exit the Jeep, but I've forgotten his bottle at home. He nuzzles my knees, begging, but all I can do is hug him and scratch his little head. Mae quickly discovers that I've brought a pail of grain and thrusts her giant head in the open hatch of the Jeep. So I drive away, slowly, hoping they will follow. This actually works pretty well for the first half mile. Then Mae becomes bored with the intermittent reward for her extended effort, and peels off into the nearest field, the calves trailing in her wake.

The next half hour is a dance rehearsal in the early morning light. My pajamas flutter behind me as I abandon the Jeep and circle the pasture on foot, trying to keep them from fleeing into the woods on the far side. After I've got her moving in the right direction again, I jog down the hill, shaking the grain bucket and trying to stay two steps ahead of the food-motivated behemoth. Harry trots along beside me, sucking on my pant leg, Lucy and Izzy bringing up the rear. We turn into my driveway and they amble into the barn as if it were any ordinary day. The calves duck into the open stall doors and fold into sleep instantly. I give Mae her bucket of grain, fill a water tub in the barn, and secure them for the foreseeable future. No one is going back out to pasture until the fence gets a few thousand more volts of electricity pulsing through it.

At the diner two hours later, Tommy says Grace and adds a thoughtful prayer of gratitude that I have recovered my adventurous, wandering cows. He's just so darn sweet.

CHAPTER TEN

October's glorious weather had arrived on the heels of a fierce nor'easter. Early. Not a good sign for the upcoming winter months. The cows have settled in as if Red Gate has always been their home. Harry has grown into a fine, fat young man. Lucy avoids me like the plague—I haven't had my hands on her since the day I brought her home. Izzy hides behind her mama, peeking around at me with wall-eyed distrust. Mae is still insistent about receiving her daily grain, and bellows like an elephant in heat if she so much as sees me move past a window. I sneak around in the dark, trying to outwit her, but she always knows. She could wake the dead with her caterwauling.

So far this has seemed like a fairly simple and bucolic process: buy cattle, bring them home, turn them out into a newly fenced pasture, and watch them graze in the sunshine while sipping a cool drink on the deck. But a word to the wise for anyone considering the pastoral peace of a herd of your own lovely cows: some of them have a wild streak and can be a little resistant about being confined. Izzy is the perfect, maddening example. She flatly refuses to stay home. She much prefers standing in the middle of the road while listening to her distraught mother bellow. It seems to bring her a certain delight, in fact.

Though Izzy is no more genetically bison than the rest of them, she leans decidedly in that species direction. I realize that in the two months she's been with me, I've never heard her moo. She grunts instead, bucks and kicks up her heels as she races around the pasture, or up the road, and she loves to butt heads with the others. It's a game they don't seem to enjoy very much.

Bison or cow, I am beginning to think of her as the devil's spawn, and for the past week, she has been mostly confined to the barn. I've fenced and re-fenced, cut brush away from the line, bought a new, powerful electric fence charger—but every time I let her out to play and graze, she heads right for the fence, crawls between the hot strands, scrambles over the stone wall, and gallops off to greener pastures. Or stands like a dim-witted sentry in the middle of the dusty road. The school bus driver is having a conniption fit and my elderly neighbors are particularly unimpressed since it is, of course, their neatly trimmed lawn that she heads for.

There are two clear and equally distasteful choices: send her to the butcher, or spend another thousand dollars to have a fence company come in and do a complete overhaul by building the bovine equivalent of Fort Knox. During calf recovery operations, which entail me panting along behind her as we zigzag back home, the butcher seems like a reasonable (even agreeable) option. But when she's safe in the barn, innocently staring at me with her liquid-brown, four-month old eyes, it's not nearly as attractive. My checkbook is about to take a serious hit, with no real guarantee of success. But, shamelessly admitted carnivore that I am, I've never been able to eat veal.

My shop is complete and I've turned my attention to exactly what I might turn my hands to while in it. Some creative force is itching to get out, but it has not yet occurred to me exactly what that is. I know it has something to do with wood, but that leaves a lot of room for interpretation and expression. In the meantime, I sort and organize my growing tool collection.

Tom and I have been going to church nearly every Sunday, and Wednesday evenings as well. I think we really are dating in church. Is this even legal? Have I turned into a middle-aged, reformed zealot? No, because all I can think of while I'm seated next to him is how to engineer another few moments alone with him. I try to keep the obsessive thoughts to a minimum, but the moment I see him my heart betrays me, somersaults in my chest, and leaves me lightheaded, gasping for oxygen.

On the other hand, Tommy has begun to studiously ignore the obvious, and I'm trying my best to keep it from being obvious. But we find ourselves almost purposely avoiding one another. It truly does remind me of hesitant, shy high school romances, where each affected party pretends that the other is almost invisible. But his laughter illuminates my day. His penetrating eyes sear my brain.

We keep it light and our growing friendship is evolving the way it should. When it's kept in this context of safety, there is an ease about us that I don't remember with other men that I've had a romantic interest in. He feels a little like a brother, or a best friend. A best friend that I'd like to see buck naked. It is almost a religious fervor, this yearning.

October is the month that Chuck Hazelton and I go striped bass fishing down the Cape. We've done it for years, stealing weekend days and nights and camping on the beaches of Race Point at the outermost reach of the sandy peninsula. We fish till our shoulders ache and our stomachs growl. And we take the opportunity to reconnect, to laugh and talk, tease each other, tell stupid jokes and long-winded, mostly true stories. His wonderful, trusting wife enjoys these weekends as well. It allows her a little time at home alone, and she's gracious beyond measure about his absence in the company of another woman.

A million years ago Chuck and I had the talk about the quality and content of our relationship, about the depth of friendship and its steadfast, platonic nature. Just so that we could avoid any confusion if it ever arose. It's pure and playful, feeds each of us with its unspoken devotion. I've never asked, but know that Chuck would do anything for me. Same here. During my long, debilitating slide into depression, something he has difficulty comprehending, Chuck never treated me like the broken, fragile bits of shell I felt like. He just took me fishing, whether I ever wet a line, or just sat like a sodden lump of clay in the sand.

On this particular fall trip, I've been smiling since we met at his house. It's almost two days later and we're sitting in front of a crackling campfire on the deserted fall beach. Chuck is thinking of the fish he reeled in, and I'm lost in a pleasant daydream about Tommy.

His gruff, rumbling voice interrupts me. "What's up with you?"

"Whadda ya mean?"

"Kinda happy, aren't you?"

"Bother you?"

"Yeah, it's downright aggravating." But his green eyes are smiling and he really wants to know.

"Don't fall off your seat or anything, but I think I might be falling in love. Maybe…."

"Yeah? With who?"

"Uh, this guy named Tom."

He sits back, stares at the fire. "Geez, Bec. I thought you loved me all these years, been pining away up on the hill."

"That's right, just forgot to mention it until now."

He nods, satisfied. "I thought so."

"Unfortunately, Cathy snagged you first. Lucky for you."

Chuck thinks for several minutes, his eyes narrowed. "This means you won't be able to go fishing anymore, right?"

"What the hell are you talking about?"

"Bec, this is the way it goes. People fall in love and disappear. Remember when you were seein' that jerk in New Jersey? Christ, I didn't see you for three years."

"Yeah, 'cause I was driving to New Jersey every weekend, it was retarded. Won't happen again like that."

"Whatever."

"No, Chuck, I won't ditch on you again, I swear."

"Uh huh …" He's quiet for several minutes. A huge seal hauls his shining, black body out of the surf onto the moonlit sand below us. "Alright, let's get it over with. Tell me about him."

"Okay. Well, he's just like you, only really good looking."

This sends him into whooping howls, and the seal huffs in disgust, retreats to the relative peace of the ocean. But the truth is that the two men are very much alike. Strong, steady men of few words, deep thought, and emotion that they rarely show. Their granite faces and hands are weathered by years of exposure to the sun, wind, and rain that they work and play in. They're both men of the earth, tethered to the simplicity and wonder of the natural world.

"He's a farmer. I knew him a long time ago. We reconnected when I went to look at his beefalo herd."

"Ah." Chuck nods and grins. "That explains the cows."

"No, it just sorta worked out that way."

"Sure it did." Chuck shakes his head. "You're whacked."

"Am not. But I'm a lot happier than I used to be."

We both stare at the flat ocean for a few minutes. Piping plovers scoot ahead of the incoming ripples, skittering before their own tiny shadows in the bright light of the full moon.

"Where do old people go on dates?" Chuck smirks and I punch him in the shoulder.

"If you must know, we go to church."

He turns and gapes at me. "Are you kiddin' me?"

"No, I'm not."

"I think that's a sin, ya know."

"Do you really?" I'm not kidding at all anymore.

"Well, I guess it depends what you do in church." He wriggles his eyebrows and I laugh, relieved. Then he's quiet for a moment. "Does this mean you gotta bring him fishing with us?"

"Probably not. He's got a real farm, too many chores. It probably won't work out."

"Good." He nods. "I like things just the way they are." He wanders off to find a convenient sand dune to piss on. When he returns he ruffles up my salt-dampened hair. "You want me to talk to him?"

"About what?"

"You know, about this …" Chuck's hand sweeps to encompass the beach and I get what he's trying to say. We've talked about it a hundred times—the assumptions people leap to when a married man and an unmarried woman spend time like this.

"No. I've already explained it to him. He's good with it."

"And does this poor sucker feel the same way about you?"

I shrug. "I really don't know … sometimes I think he does."

"He's a damn fool if he doesn't."

"Aw, Chuck, that was awful sweet."

"Yeah, whatever." He frowns, digs his toes in the sand. "We're not gonna go through another blues period if this doesn't work out, right?"

"No. I promise."

"Good. It was a real pain in the ass."

This has been an extraordinarily long and personal

conversation for a man who keeps his own counsel, and prefers when others do the same. What he *meant* to say was that he loves me and doesn't want me to get hurt. I know this and don't need to say it, just as he didn't need to. It's a given.

CHAPTER ELEVEN

My herd is no longer exclusively bovine. I've added a horse to the mix, something I'd promised myself that I wouldn't do again, but there you have it—the best laid plans of mice and men can be completely obliterated at a moment's notice. After battling cancer for the past eight years, a dear friend of mine has received a distressing diagnosis. David's four horses must find homes immediately, and his uppermost concern is that they go to folks who will love and care for them.

This particular horse is a teenage gelding, a Percheron/Pinto cross, though he looks more like a cross between a Holstein and a bulldozer. His curvy little ears make him really adorable, in an endearing, hulking sort of way. I'd ridden him several times over the last year with David, while we reconnected on the trails surrounding his home, laughing and telling stories, riding in the snow until our toes and noses froze.

He's been called "Hardy" all his life, but since his primary purpose in life is uninterrupted consumption, and he's lazy as a doorstop, and will never, ever be svelte, I call him Piglet. He's never been without the company of other horses, and he's never been pastured with cows. So on the first day at my farm, I turn him out in the large, fenced backyard. He nibbles nervously at the grass, and pounds up and down the fence line, watching the cows in the pasture and calling to them in shrill, anxious whinnies. He's lonely and would really like to be buddies, but Mae is decidedly uninterested in him, keeps her band of calves a safe distance from the odd, black and white creature. She's trying to work out exactly what he is, and what his questionable intentions might be, before she takes a chance with her precious charges.

On the third day, when Piglet has sufficiently calmed himself and accepted his new circumstances, and Mae has decided he poses no serious threat, I turn him out to the pasture. This shocking development spooks her, particularly since Piglet is enthusiastically trotting toward the bovine band. Mae directs one abbreviated, urgent moo at her troops and flees into the thick woods at the bottom of the pasture, the calves crashing through the saplings behind her. Piglet is unwilling to brave the tangled thicket and gallops around the pasture calling to them. Mae is not sympathetic. She stays in there for two days, emerging only when Piglet has been safely tucked into his stall at night. But by the third day, they have negotiated an uneasy truce—he grazes on one side of the pasture, and she and the calves graze on the other. At the end of a week, they have finally become an integrated herd, and we can all relax.

If the cows ever escape again, it'll make my job a lot easier to track them down from horseback and herd them home, assuming that Piglet doesn't escape with them. In the meantime, my hay bill is going to ratchet into the red zone.

Today, on the way home from church, Tommy finally reached over and held my hand, for the briefest moment. Big step. The warmth of his palm, the firm strength of his grasp made me goosey. I was wise enough not to remark on it, or perhaps just struck dumb for a moment. Loss of speech doesn't happen to me very often, and when I'd recovered, we went seamlessly on about the bible passages that the pastor had presented for discussion. This is when we do our best talking. The rest of what little time we spend together, we're usually debating the merits of various livestock feeds or working.

Tom and his father have a small sawmill on the farm. They produce most of the lumber needed for their farm, and some specialty jobs for local craftsmen and carpenters. Occasionally I step in to help, not because I'm asked, but because it gives me an opportunity to be with him. The only conversation that takes place is in the form of direction and purpose.

"Grab the end of that board, Bec."

"Yes, sir!" I take hold of the newly milled plank and salute him. Tom was a marine before he was a wild man, before he was a reformed wild man. And he must have been a boy scout because he's always prepared, always thinking his way through the next strategic move. His economy of motion is beautiful to watch.

We work for another couple hours. Eyebrow lifts, chin tips, and head tilts are the communication we use when the mill is running and one could not be heard above its screech and whine.

He flips the switch and the saw blade stops. "Lunch?"

"Sure, what have you got?"

"Only the best for you, my dear."

I try not to swoon or read too much into the casual endearment as Tom pulls two peanut butter sandwiches out of a brown paper bag. We sit in the October sun and share a half gallon of cold well water, swallow the peanut butter and homemade jam. He perches across from me on a tractor bucket. I've found a convenient stump.

"Nice, huh?"

"Best sandwich I've had in years, Tom."

"I can cook, you know." He grins at me. "You wanna stay for supper?"

"I can't. Jack's home tonight, and he might need a bowl of soup or something."

Tom nods. "How's he doing?"

"Better than me." I feel the tears behind my eyes. In the weeks since Jack moved in, I've been witness to his daily pain. And the astonishing fact that he never complains.

Tom stands up and moves past me, laying a hand on my shoulder as he goes. "You're a good woman." This is his best compliment. It means far more than if he'd said I was pretty, or looked especially nice in my grubby jeans and sweaty t-shirt. "God is close in this, you know."

"I know."

He grunts and moves on. "This tree won't cut itself. Are you going to sit there all day?" Less than ten minutes have passed.

"I think I need a nap." He ignores me and moves to the brain of the mill. "Can I run it, Tommy?"

"No."

"How come? It's not rocket science, you know."

"Obviously," he grins. "But if you got hurt, I'd never forgive myself. Then I'd have to cart you to the hospital, and it would really slow things down."

I move to my position. "Well, what if the blade snaps while I'm standing here?"

"Then it would be all bloody and I'd have to replace it."

"Ah …"

The next two hours pulse by, counted by the long, clean planks that drop off the squared trees. The heady scent of pine engulfs us in its powdery sawdust. At three o'clock Tom switches the mill off and we walk down the hill towards the barn.

I head for my Jeep. "See you later."

"Wait up. I have something for you." He ducks into the barn. When he returns he is holding a beautiful, gleaming wooden bowl. "Dad made this for you."

I take the bowl, turning it in my hands, admiring the craftsmanship. "Really?"

"Uh huh."

Then he leans forward and kisses me. His lips barely brush over mine, and the smell of sharp pine and sweet cut grass assails me, addles my already twisted brain. He brushes a stray speck of sawdust off my cheek, and then he turns and walks away. My knees wobble as I get into the Jeep and turn it for home. That kiss had to last longer than I would have liked. Three minutes would have been longer than I liked!

On Sunday we were back to our normal church-going routine. He didn't even hold my hand in the car. But he smiled and laughed and it didn't matter at all. When we returned to the farm, Tom's father was outside tending a smoking grill. I waved to him and he motioned me over.

"Hi, Earl. What's cooking?"

"Dinner. You staying?"

In farm family vernacular "dinner" is the midday and largest meal, particularly on Sundays. Supper is the evening meal, light and easy to sleep on. I glanced at Tom and he nodded.

"Sure, if you'll have me."

Earl lifted the grill hood and basted the duck that sizzled on the rack. Its heavenly scent reached my nostrils, drawing me closer. I was nearly drooling in anticipation. Earl smiled. The picnic table was set with plates and silverware—well, set like a man does it. Everything was piled in a heap at one end. I went to set it properly and Tom disappeared into the house. He returned moments later with a steaming bean pot and placed it on the table.

"Did you make those?" I asked.

"No, the tooth fairy did. Sit."

I sat. Earl brought the crispy, glistening duck to the table and we said a hasty, hungry Grace. Then we ate that splendid meal and savored the Indian Summer warmth of a late October afternoon. The trees around the edges of the pasture glowed in the midday sun. I glowed in my heart. It was obvious that these two bachelor farmers had planned the meal in advance, and I've not had better in years. Dessert was a blackberry pie with vanilla ice cream. I knew they did not indulge in these treats very often on their own.

"You guys eat like this every day?"

Tommy's lips twitched in a teasing smirk. "But of course. You don't think we did this for you?"

"No, of course not." I smiled back at him.

Earl shook his gray head and stood. He squeezed my shoulder with his strong, broad hand and left.

"What's up with him?"

"It's his way of saying you're part of the farm."

"Oh. Well, thank you."

"Mmmm." Tom's eyes sparkled at me.

Tommy's farm in the red-gold glory of October.

For countless years I'd cried only when threatened with my own imminent death, or in anger or frustration, occasionally from the effects of overwork and fatigue, and only when absolutely alone. It revealed weakness as far as I concerned, not something I was willing to allow others to witness. Church and the pastor have reminded me of what I was so afraid of, that I don't have to control everything all of the time. I am loved by God, cradled in the everlasting security of that love. It's my choice to move into it or to move away from it. And it's perfectly fine to show that I care for others. In fact, it's imperative that I do.

Now I find myself standing in the door yard of Tom and Earl's farm with tears dripping off my chin, while he watches, smiling. He steps in to me, thumbs a tear off my cheek, then kisses the spot gently.

That did it. I *knew* I was in love … with both of them.

Farmer's love is quiet. It doesn't shout from the rooftops or dance till midnight. It doesn't make grand, gaudy gestures or heady proclamations. It serves duck and baked beans, and warm blackberry pie. And then it serves up more work.

CHAPTER TWELVE

November passed without measurable snow. Swirling flurries teased at what was to come, and the cattle took the warning seriously. They began to inhale entire bales of hay as if they were nothing more than air—free air! As if there were a cheap, limitless supply, which there was not. And if they just ate the damn stuff that would be enough to frighten me. But they don't. They tromp around on it, poop on it, sleep on it, and turn their discriminating noses up at the sodden result. Then Mae bellows for a fresh load.

About this point it occurs to me that I may have been somewhat addled in July, intoxicated with the glorious abundance of summer and waist-high grass when I leapt from ground zero to five, in livestock terms. Starbuck is off with his adoptive mother in the forest, abundantly rich with acorns this year, and Harry is the smallest fraction of the hay guzzling herd. One blustery afternoon, while I'm driving to the grain store and reminding myself to call the hay dealer in the morning, I tally up what I've spent since the beginning of this adventure. Big mistake, and I mentally click the "delete" button. Best not to think about it.

Jack's disease progresses every day. Still he doesn't complain, but I can hear him moaning in the night. In the morning his eyes are red-rimmed from lack of restful sleep. I only cry for him when he's not around to see. It has nothing to do with control, and everything to do with making his life here in my home, his last home, as comfortable as possible.

My annual early December vacation to the Caribbean was drawing near. I didn't see how I could leave him all alone, and he wasn't strong enough to tend the cows. Tom told me to go, said he would do the chores and keep an eye on Jack. So I went.

The crystal Caribbean water and the drenching, dark green of the rainforest soothed my tired soul, pampered and nourished me for ten days. I luxuriated under its calming influence, drank more rum than I should have, danced till well past midnight when the opportunity arose, went sailing, snorkeling, and never even thought of home. Almost. One of the island men that I've known for years made a determined and flattering attempt at courting me, and quite honestly, I considered it. It wouldn't have been a sticky complication, wouldn't have followed me home to the frozen hinterland, but when all was said and done, I just couldn't.

Damn, I thought as I walked back to my tent cottage alone, *he's really got hold of me.*

When I returned to the frigid northeast, tanned and restored late on Monday night, Tom's truck was in the driveway. A foot of snow had fallen while I was gone and the driveway had been plowed, the walk and deck had been shoveled. Wood smoke curled from the chimney, the only hint of warmth and promise in the frigid night. The lights were off, but a candle flickered on the kitchen counter and it glowed warmly as I entered, shivering in my light, tropic clothes. Ropes of fresh evergreen adorned the beams, reminding me that Christmas was just around the corner.

I heard the bedsprings creak overhead, then his feet padding along the floor to the head of the stairs.

"That you, Becca?"

"No. It's Santa Claus."

He came down the stairs, wearing a t-shirt and boxers. It was the least amount of clothing I'd ever seen him in, and I tried not to stare. Sort of. He caught me in a warm, welcome hug.

"What did you bring me?"

I kissed him on the cheek. "How's Jack?"

"He's okay, resting now."

"You stayed here?"

"Just tonight. Didn't want you to come home to a cold house."

"Cows okay?"

"Yup, just ducky." His hands rested on my shoulders and his eyes glimmered in the light from the candle. God, he looked good. "You tired, Bec?"

"Uh huh, long day. It's pretty cold here."

Tom laughed. "Ya think?"

"Where's Tug?" The dog had not come to wiggle around my knees the way he usually did.

"He's sleeping with Jack. Hasn't left his side since you went."

"Oh. Go back to bed, Tommy. I'm sorry I woke you."

He grinned. "Where you gonna sleep?"

"I'll sleep on the couch." I was so tired I could barely stand.

"Yuh, sure." He took my hand and led me up the stairs. Another candle glowed on the windowsill of my bedroom.

"Did we lose power?"

"Yesterday. Good thing you've got the woodstove." Tom sat on the edge of the bed and pulled me into him, warming my arms with his big hands. "You're freezing."

"Not used to it. It's been eighty-five degrees in my world for the last ten days. This is brutal."

"Poor baby." he crooned.

"What about Jack's end of the house? There's no woodstove out there."

"Brought a kerosene heater from the farm. He's fine." Tom had unbuttoned my loose cotton blouse. "Come to bed. I'll keep you warm."

"Okay." I'd been up since before dawn in St. John. Taxi, ferry, taxi, plane, another plane, a bus, and a forty-five-minute drive later, it was well past midnight. I was so tired that I wasn't really processing what was happening.

Tommy lay back on the bed and I got in on my side. He pulled the down comforter up to my chin and wrapped his arm around my shoulder. I shivered for a moment and he held me tighter. As the warmth began to penetrate, I started to drift off to sleep. I heard Tom giggle and it pulled me back to a vague semblance of consciousness.

"What?"

"You're pretty funny. I'm trying to make love to you and you're falling asleep."

"Huh?" His hand was on my hip and his lips brushed my neck. And then sleep was the furthest thing from my mind.

"Tommy, it's been a wicked long time since … you know."

"We could go bike riding if you want, but I think you'll remember." He smiled softly.

"Is this a sin?" I asked him in the dark.

"Yeah, if you don't do it right." His body was pressed along mine and his calloused hands moved like liquid fire over my back.

"Tommy …"

"Hush, now."

Farmer's love is slow and easy. It takes its time and doesn't rush things. It's hard and hot and delicious, like wild blueberry pancakes with real maple syrup. It comes in the winter when the hay is in and the woodstove is full, and it lays its tender, perfect hands on your heart and doesn't let go.

Red Gate Farm dressed in winter white.

CHAPTER THIRTEEN

Jack is dying in earnest now, treating it like a job that must be done well. Christmas has come and gone, and the hardest, longest stretch of winter is lying stark and white before us. My daughter joined us for Christmas dinner and she laughed with Jack and Tom until late in the evening. Men in their forties and fifties, whether facing death or religion, still respond to a pretty young woman with flattery and flirtation. I enjoyed it as much as she did, and she held her own, charming them thoroughly with wit and intelligence.

On her way up to bed she took me aside. "Finally, Mum, you found a good one."

"You mean Jack?"

"Yeah, that's exactly what I meant." She shakes her head and hugs me. "Don't screw it up."

Children can always be depended upon for that sorely needed vote of confidence.

The tree has been dragged out of the living room and set up in the snow. Frozen, peanut butter-slathered pine cones dangle from it to feed the birds. Jack sits in the window watching them, part of every day. He tells me humorous stories from his adventurous life, talks about the places he'd still like to see. He reads. He sleeps. He cuddles his dogs and whispers in their velvet ears.

One night at supper he tells me that he doesn't want to die in the winter.

"You mean because they won't be able to bury you?"

"No. I mean because I want to see another spring. I'd rather die while the world is coming back to life." He pauses. "It will help the others cope."

"No it won't." There is a long, heavy pause.

"Well, I like to think it will." His thin face stretches into a lopsided grin. "If there's any sobbing at my funeral, I'll come back to haunt every last one of you."

"Okay." I walk back into the kitchen, my breath knotted in my chest. How can he smile and tease when I say something dopey like that?

Tom seems to understand it. He comes over late in the afternoon sometimes and sits to play cribbage with Jack. I go out to the barn and leave them with their conversation. The cows and Piglet are glad to see me, or at least the fresh batch of hay I toss at them. Harry licks my hand with sloppy affection. I listen to them chewing for awhile and then wander into the workshop. Tommy joins me after an hour.

"He okay?"

"Yup. Resting." He picks up the picture frame I'm working on. It has birch bark trim on the face, and tiny strips of twigs fastening it down to the wood backing. "This is good."

"Thanks." And suddenly I'm crying and Tom is rocking me in his arms, his heavy hands patting my back.

"It's okay, Bec. He knows it's God's plan for him"

"I know he knows, but it still makes me angry. Why him?"

"Why not?" he asks.

"Because he doesn't deserve this?" My lower lip is trembling and I'm about to lose it and spew venom all over the shop.

"I know, but it's his to carry. And he's doin' one hell of a job with it." Tom brushes the hair away from my face and kisses me. "You need a good night's sleep."

I turn back to the workbench, take the hammer from its rack, and pound on a piece of maple. He leans on the bench, watching me until I run out of steam.

"Feel better?"

"No."

Tommy disappears up the loft stairs. I hear him moving hay bales around and wonder what he's doing. He goes back out through the barn and his footsteps crunch on the snow. He returns a few minutes later, carrying pillows and my down comforter.

"Come up with me."

I drop the hammer and follow him. The cows are munching hay below us. Tom flourishes a hand at the makeshift hay fort that he's constructed. He fluffs up the fragrant bale that he's opened. Then he spreads a blanket on it, throws the pillows down, and finishes with the comforter on top.

"Take your jacket off and get in."

I do as he says and he lies down beside me, the solid length of his warm body pressed against my back. And then he starts to hum under his breath, deep in his chest.

"Becca, there's only two things in this life that God gives us to choose from. Love and Fear." He warms me with his hands. "Which one are you going to choose?"

My anger is still right on the surface, but it's dissipating from the heart of me. I can feel it going, a slurry of cool mercury and hot blood draining away. "When did you get so damn smart?"

"You mean you never noticed? I thought you loved me because I'm brilliant."

"No. I love you because you're crazy."

"Yeah. Crazy about you ..."

It's the first time we've said the "L" word, at least to each other. And it didn't hurt in the slightest. No one panicked, no one scrambled to cover an awkward faux pas. It rests easy between us. It rests like a tiny hummingbird in summer, an iridescent, feathered jewel filled with sweet nectar.

CHAPTER FOURTEEN

March holds on to winter like it's afraid to lose its icy grasp on a familiar lover. I hold onto Tom in what I can only hope is a more gracious, thoughtful manner. It's not, but I like to imagine that I'm capable of that. And Jack holds onto life, waiting for the first swollen buds on the sugar maples. He turns his face to the warming sun, lost in his own thoughts. I bring him steaming herbal tea and honey, which he no longer drinks to the bottom. His system is shutting down, his organs hardening to stone in the sunken cavities of his thin, pain-ravaged body.

He no longer plays cribbage with Tom. Sometimes they talk, more often they don't. They just sit and watch the winter untangle its frozen knot. The cows stir restlessly in their stalls, heads held high in the morning, scenting the warming breeze that flows across the quilted pasture.

One afternoon Jack calls to me from his living room. I race to see what he needs, my heart in my throat.

"Look …" he gasps, pointing. "Fog!"

"Uh huh?"

"Spring, it's almost here." He coughs, gathers the blanket around his shoulders, and falls asleep.

Piglet snorts at the cows, pushes them around the bales of hay I've thrown out, herds them into the corner of the pasture just because he can, stands watch over the calves as they sleep. Piglet will live out the rest of his days in my pasture, while his former owner, David, lives out the rest of his.

I'm beginning to tire, not of the farm and its related chores, but of the steady march of dying people who seem to find me, or I them. I wonder if this is what the rest of my life will consist of, and I struggle to understand what God, or Fate, or something else I can't understand, has placed before me. Finally I give up, or rather supplicate, and just accept that this is His plan. Not without a significant quantity of bitter, scalding tears and gnashing of teeth, and certainly not with an abundance of grace. But I try.

My pastor, his wife, and the entire congregation surround me every Sunday and Wednesday with prayers and support, and I suddenly realize that this is all part of the tapestry that's been woven around me. I found this church and this community in the nick of time. They will all help me find the right way to assist and comfort the people that I love and will shortly lose, those that are facing the ultimate destiny we all must. They are simply facing it right now.

April comes early with a warm, wet wind. The snow banks melt in a matter of days, and the grass underneath is matted in long, stringy twists of pale brown. I go out to rake when the lion's share of the moisture is leached from the ground. Jack watches from the window. When I next look up he's sitting on the deck, wrapped in that blanket. The dogs are lying at his feet, watching me.

Tommy comes over for dinner that night, but Jack is too weak and tired to join us. He can't weigh more than eighty pounds now, and Tom picks him up easily, carries him to bed. Jack turns his face away from Tom's broad shoulder, accepting the help and disengaging from him in the same moment, leaning on his own dignity, struggling to maintain a sense of independence that has long since fled. This breaks my heart clean in two. When Tom comes back downstairs, I don't have a lot to say and he pats my hand, frowns at me.

"Is this too much for you?"

"No. Do you think it is?"

"Sometimes I worry about you—it's taking a lot out of you, I think."

"Not too much."

He watches me for a moment, wondering if I'll cry. "I think you should come to church this Sunday. Sometimes we all need a little spiritual nourishment."

I haven't been going to church lately. On my two days off a week I think I should be close at hand if Jack needs something, which he rarely does.

"All right."

Tommy nods, satisfied. "I'll pick you up."

"Don't need to, I can meet you there."

"No, Bec. I'll pick you up."

I've started to retreat, and I know he feels it. He's not in a panic about it, and he doesn't smother me and push me into flight or anger. But he feels me slipping away. It has recently occurred to me that when Jack is gone, Tom and I will have some choices to make. Not right away, but not that far off either. At this point it's fairly clear that we have chosen one another, and that it's not a passing fling. It never was. But at the beginning of a romance, even a slow, tentative one like ours, one doesn't ponder these things. Or their implications.

By now I've lived in this house for fifteen years. It's my home, the place that I have been happiest and most settled in. And Tom has lived in his house, at the farm, on and off throughout his whole life. More on than off. His elderly, widowed father is there, and his work and his livestock. I can see where this is going if I let it, and despite myself, despite the love I feel for this kind, tough, sweet man, I'm also feeling a tight, nasty edge of resentment.

Why would I have to move? Why would *my* life

have to change? And what about all the things I love that surround my daily movements: My grandmother's paintings, the pictures of my parents, family antiques that I've faithfully lugged with me everywhere I've gone. My dishes and books and fishing rods. Tommy's house is packed with the things that generations of his family have accumulated. What about Tug? There are no dogs at the farm and I wonder if they've decided not to have any.

Tom is stretched out on the rug in front of the woodstove. He's staring into the fire and I wonder what he's thinking. But I don't ask. Conversation between us has dwindled of late. The future is sticking its masked, unknowable face into our unsettled present.

I stand off the couch. "Going to bed. You coming?"

"No, I think I'll go home." Even his use of the word "home" rankles my nerves.

"Fine." I go into the bathroom and shut the door. And I sit on the closed toilet seat and cry in frustrated privacy. I hear the back door open and close and he's gone. We've had our first fight and no one raised their voice.

Even farmer's fights are quiet. Silence and peace are two very different things. Is this really what I want?

CHAPTER FIFTEEN

Jack got the spring he wished for, one of the best we'd had in years. He died at the summer equinox. Purple lupine and pink peonies were in full bloom, and the air that day was light and cool. Liz sat with him for his last hours. They were peaceful hours for Jack, and he was ready to relinquish this life for the painless freedom of the other side. She took his keening dogs when she left, and suddenly the house is far too still and empty.

After the funeral, I spend three days in the barn, with the cows coming and going out the wide back door. They stare at me with their liquid-brown eyes. They lick my face with rough, slobbery tongues, tasting the salt of my tears. Mae is quiet, not bellowing for her grain, observing the silence of grief. Piglet nudges my shoulder, blowing softly in my face. Tug curls into the corner on a pile of loose hay and doesn't move. It's as if the world has slowed and quieted to mark his passing, but of course, it hasn't. Tom stops to check on me and there's nothing to say to him. He somehow understands, or maybe he doesn't, but he leaves me to my pain.

I never really thought that I could save him—in fact, I knew that no one could. My only intention was to make his last months more comfortable. But it wasn't nearly enough and now he's gone.

By the following Sunday I have pulled myself together enough to put on reasonably clean clothes and drive to church. And I sit beside Tom, whose eyes lit with transparent pleasure and relief as he watched me come in. His hand rests on my knee while we listen to the pastor. Tom asks for a prayer of remembrance for Jack's departed soul. I can feel the congregation's loving intent to comfort me—it enfolds me in compassion and sympathy. The Lord's Prayer is spoken in a hundred voices, lifted as one, ringing off the white, plaster walls. The fellowship hour after service is a gauntlet of human beings and their individual voices, and after thirty minutes I have to go. It is more than enough and never enough at the same time.

Tommy walks beside me to the car. "Do you want to come back to the farm?"

"Thanks. I can't today."

"Becca, you did your best … and you did it well." We're only standing two feet apart, but the distance is immeasurable and immense.

"I know. I'll talk to you soon."

"I'll be there."

Immediately I am filled with regret that I didn't go to the farm, but I have nothing to say, nothing that will bridge the growing gap between us. With Jack gone, there is only the question of where Tom and I are going in this relationship, and right now it's too much to consider.

A week passes, maybe two. Tommy appears at the door to the shop, catching me off guard and vulnerable. I'm working on a new project and he watches me for a little while.

"Becca, are you ever coming back?"

It's a fair question and I can't look at him. "I don't know."

He steps around the bench and traps me in the corner. "What is it?"

"I don't know."

"Yes, you do. Tell me." He stands looking into my eyes with the intense blue gaze that I used to melt in.

I shrug. "I … just can't right now."

"Have your feelings for me changed?"

Another fair question and I almost hate him for it. "No …"

"Okay. That's all I need to know. I'll be there when you're ready." He kisses me on the forehead and leaves.

I sit on an overturned bucket and sob for an hour. *Damn him.*

I've been alone for these past seven years by choice. Before that, my romantic life had been one frustrating relationship after another, always choosing the wrong man, always ending with pain and sorrow. Somewhere in my heart I knew that I needed a reprieve. The habit of stealing energy from others had gotten me nowhere, left me bereft and lonely in its wake. I needed to be alone and learn to find contentment in that, find my own peace that was not constructed around the needs or desires of another human being. But giving up any addiction, whether drugs or alcohol, or one that disguises itself as something imitating love, is hard, lonely work.

Maybe that's where the cows came in—they need me, but there's nothing complicated or confusing in our relationship. I provide them with a safe place to graze, and watching them provides me with peace and contentment. I feed them, they eat. I clean up after them, they produce more to clean up. It's a predictable routine with few surprises. But back to the troublesome point—human relationships.

I purposely chose celibacy, but it wasn't always easy, and it didn't come naturally. Sure, I had a few temptations along the way, even one obsessive crush that played itself out over several unconsummated years. Those are often the best kind—you can be in some remote semblance of love without the daily reality and responsibility of caring for someone. The object of your infatuation is nothing more than an ideal, one that never disappoints, until the end when you finally grow bored of all that unfulfilled yearning and hate them for it. The breakups are not nearly as messy as a real relationship—in fact, no one knows but you.

In contrast, this developing whatever-it-is with Tom leaves me confused and conflicted. It is perched right on the precarious edge of impending reality. Do I really want this? Yes, on the one hand, I do. The comfort and companionship beckon, woo me with warmth and promise. The previous failures haunt me. The mistakes multiply in my mind until they are all I can recall. If Tommy knows what's good for him, he'll stay on his farm and thank the Lord that he was spared.

He calls one early August morning. The sun is barely over the trees on the east side of the pasture.

"Remember last year when you told me about the gratitude practice?"

"Yes."

"Are you still doing it?"

"Uh, no."

"You should. I love you."

He hangs up and I sit on the deck staring into the golden ball of light that nearly blinds me. Tug is lying at my feet. The cows are grazing in the pasture. Izzy, Lucy, and Harry are bunched up in the corner where the stone wall disappears into the dark green of the woods. Mae moos to her new calf, who blatantly ignores her. I realize that I haven't named the new herd member.

It's a heifer, so I'll call her Jackie.

CHAPTER SIXTEEN

One early Sunday morning I was cleaning the barn, scrubbing the slimy layer of green algae from the walls of the water tank. As I guarded the hose from curious noses during the ten-minute refill, I turned my thoughts to what I was going to do about church, and just not on that particular day.

I've been struggling with the doctrinal issues that our pastor has been dwelling on, almost pounding the pulpit with lately. When I was a teenager I'd turned away from the church over these very same themes, primarily because of their unyielding, rigid nature. Back then I discovered that I just didn't fit into a church body, or it seemed, organized religion of any kind. Each one proclaimed their own brand of "the way," and vehement proclamations that theirs was the *only* way. I found that exclusive righteousness odd and disconcerting.

If we, the entire human race, are all God's children, then exactly which singular, narrow human interpretation and tradition of worship can be declared the only right one? Though it was not the focused or final reason, that personal discomfort within a church body had contributed to my eventual retreat from God. But blaming organized religion alone would be cheating.

There was also the small matter of losing my first true love in a tragic accident when I was a very young woman. Having no skills to deal with that senseless loss, and having made the brilliant decision to keep it to myself, the only obvious choice was to blame Paul's death on either me or God. So I did both. Instead of grief, I opted for Guilt and Anger, in relatively equal depth and measure. I can tell you, it was a stupendously poor choice and I have paid for it dearly.

Thirty years later, I'd finally found my way back through my own spiritual exploration, and it was in that spirit that I'd sought the company of others, imagining that I was now mature enough to listen and learn without the spectacular, know-it-all judgment of adolescence and early adulthood.

But the last couple sermons had been particularly loaded with strict doctrinal messages of hell and damnation for the unsaved, and further, that the privilege of Heaven and basking in the brilliant light of God's presence after our deaths is granted *only* to those of us in this specific denomination of Christians—the true believers. It was the first time this had come up since my attendance at this church, or maybe I wasn't paying close enough attention to less-blatant messages, distracted as I was with falling in love with Tom, and the dying people all around me.

Startled, I'd glanced around at the gathered parishioners. Everyone seemed to be nodding and whispering amens with devoted zeal, and it had come over me … no, not a dawning of re-born faith, but a nagging reminder of my youthful protest of this precise message. Each of us must discover our own spiritual truths, and mine are remarkably different. It was suddenly and abundantly clear that I was once again the misfit. I seemed to be the sole dissenter in a sea of believers, confidently assured of their place in Heaven, and more importantly, their free pass from the everlasting fires of Hell. Tommy wasn't present on this particular Sunday, so I couldn't look to see his reaction. But I did look towards the pulpit, and I found the pastor staring at me, just about boring holes in me.

He *knows*, I thought. He knows I am the heathen traitor in their midst! I would have slunk out then, past the pews and the enraptured faces, but it only would have drawn unwanted attention. On the off chance that they're right, and I am indeed condemned to burn in endless agony, I'd rather my passage be a private matter.

On Tuesday, after careful consideration, I wrote a long e-mail to the Pastor, explaining that I'd been having difficulty with doctrine and the absolute, literal translation of the Bible. From my heart I thanked him for the support and prayers that have been offered. And then I told him that it was pretty clear I don't belong in this congregation. I have no desire to deceive by omission and pretend just to fit in. He replied with grace, kindness, and patience, all the while holding the firm line. And he commented that everyone struggles with doctrine from time to time, but that it is *the way*. There is no other.

I sighed to myself. They were lost to me, or more accurately, I was lost to them. I have always believed that there are unlimited paths to the Divine, none more right than another, and that each journey is at least as unique as the individual embarking on it. The rigidity of their doctrine has simply reminded me of what I'd always known. I'm not saying that I'm right and they're wrong. I'm just saying that I know what *feels* right for me. I guess we'll all find out, eventually.

However, I had a sneaking suspicion that my recent, non-conformist revelation might spell the end for Tom and me. My heart spiraled and sank, but it is what it is, and I can't pretend for him either. Clearly, that would be wrong, and I don't need the Bible to point it out.

I thought that would be the end of it, that the choice I'd made about this church would bring unavoidable collateral damage, a weird form of sinless excommunication. I would just retreat into my solitary, hedonistic background, and Tommy would fade out. Exit stage left. But I wasn't looking forward to the conversation that we would have to have about all of it. Even though I was still straddling the fence on this relationship, I was less than enthusiastic about watching him turn away over, of all things, his faith. But it's been happening for centuries—religious beliefs creating distance and rifts between individuals, communities, entire cultures, and nations. Therein lies the rub, at least for me.

I may be repeating myself, but it bears repeating. How can God, or whatever you choose to call that which is infinitely greater than yourself, separate people? But to imagine that our feelings for one another would be enough to ignore something that seems so vitally important to Tom, would be nothing less than foolish naiveté. *Damn. It's over*, I thought.

I successfully avoided Tommy for weeks, stopped eating breakfast at the diner, scanned every parking lot around town for his car before pulling in. It wasn't that I didn't want to see him—I ached to see him, to get lost in those bright blue eyes, and let his contagious laugh make my heart sing. It was the conversation I was avoiding—I hate goodbyes, particularly those I'm going to regret, that are going to hurt like the devil. Already grieving for our slim, lost chance at ever-after happiness, I moped around my little farm, not even fit for my own company. The cows looked upbeat and energetic compared to me, even in the pouring rain.

It had been raining for the better part of a month. The grass was long and shaggy, too wet to mow, and the previously perky flowers were rotting in the garden, their faces bent to the soggy soil. The pasture benefited from the late summer deluge, but the paddock behind the barn was a stinking morass of shin-deep mud and manure. The animals slogged through it to the barn and water tank, adding another layer of sticky goop to their splattered hides on each trip. Piglet was beginning to look like a stubby, brown dinosaur.

During one brief, sunny interlude, I decided to do something about it. I'd studied the paddock from every angle and knew what was needed—someone was going to have to dig a few trenches toward the downhill slope, and drain the standing water away from the flat area outside the barn doors. I looked around with furtive hope, but there was only one candidate with both motivation and opposable thumbs.

I pulled on my oldest, grubbiest pair of jeans and slipped my bare feet into rubber muck boots. If I was very careful, I might be able to keep the mud from squishing over the tops. Carrying a shovel and a garden hoe, I took a deep breath and stepped into the quagmire. Tug sat inside the barn door, declining to put his sparkling white paws into the slop. He gave me the head tilt and frown, as if to say "You've *really* lost your mind now. By the way, when's supper?"

I told him to mind his own business, and got to work. After nearly an hour of sweating, sliding, digging, and pushing my way through a ton or so of brown and green slime, I'd made progress. The water was flowing down a half-dozen foot-wide trenches, pooling at the bottom of the short hill at the base of the manure pile. The cows and Piglet had convened just beyond, watching with dumb curiosity. I was standing at the top edge of the hill, admiring my work when Tug whined and gave a short yip.

"Unless you're going to help, shut up." I told him, not bothering to turn around.

"Well, that's not very friendly."

Tom's voice and amused chuckle shot right up my spine. Startled, I spun around, recalling just an instant too late that keeping my feet firmly planted was a requirement of this particular task. So it shouldn't have been a great shock when my muck boots whizzed past my head, or when I landed in the biggest, greenest cow flap that a single cow had ever manufactured. But it was a shock, and if I hadn't knocked the wind out of myself, I'd have been screaming bloody murder right about then. I heard Tommy's gasp and hoot and then I disappeared over the lip of the hill, sliding on my back with increasing velocity toward the poop pond I'd just created.

Tug was barking like a madman. It was the last thing I heard before landing with a huge brown splash in the cesspool, my head staying just above water and coming to rest on the bank of the manure pile. *This is just perfect*, I thought.

Tommy was standing at the top of the hill, his mouth agape, and for a moment there was dead silence as we stared at each other. He tried. I really believe he tried, but there was simply no possible way he was going to avoid laughing his fool head off. I would have. I would have howled till I wet my pants. But oh, that's right, my pants were already quite wet, thank you. So I lay there like a big, poopy fish, flopping around trying to right myself, while Tommy bent over double, hands on his knees, until he'd laughed himself out.

"Stay there, Bec. I'll come get you," he offered, giggling.

"Stay here? Where'm I gonna go?" I flopped and splashed again, just to make my point. "What are you doing here, anyway?"

Tom tilted his head, grinned. "Well, I came over to see if you'd go to supper with me. But I don't think you're dressed for it."

"Funny, Tom." But I smiled back at him. I'm not sure he could tell because mucky water was running down my face at the time.

"Bec, I'll get a rope and pull you outta there, okay?"

"Sure, take your time." He hooted again, then ducked into the barn. Mae and Harry meandered to the edge of the pool. "Don't even think about coming in here," I told them. Harry was considering it, I could tell. So, things could get worse I reminded myself.

Tommy returned with a fifty-foot extension cord. "I couldn't find any rope—this'll have to do."

"Is it plugged in?"

"Of course. That way we can get you dried off at the same time." He swung the cord and tossed it with admirable precision. It landed right beside me, so I took a greasy, grimy hold of it, and with Tommy supplying the anchorage, was able to pull myself to an unsteady standing position.

"Okay," he instructed, "now I'll just keep a steady tension, and you walk yourself up outta there."

It sounded easy enough, but there were numerous false starts, slips and slides until I was free from the pond, and there was still the uphill climb. I stopped to rest for a moment.

"Bec? Want me to come down there for you?"

"I wouldn't if I were you. We'll both end up back in the pond."

"Yeah, you're right. Well, are you gonna stand there all day?"

"Shut up, Tom." Hand over hand I started up the slope, placing each foot with caution, digging in until I knew it was secure.

"Bec, you know what?"

"What?"

"You look really pretty." He grinned.

"When I get up there, I'm going to slug you." Two more steps and I'd made it. I stood huffing and puffing on relatively stable ground. Tommy stood quietly, winding the muddy extension cord up.

"So, you want to go for dinner?" he asked.

"Sure, let me just freshen up a bit." Tom chuckled and I considered wiping the smile off his clean face. The mud had found its way to mid-calf, and his arms and hands were black with slime. "You don't look so great yourself. I think we better make it another day."

"No, I'll tell you what. I'll go home and grab a couple steaks and clean up, and that'll give you time to shower and change. We can have a barbecue right here."

"All right. Give me an hour."

Tommy grinned. "Sure thing, Stinky"

I stripped naked on the deck, and threw every last piece of clothing into a hefty bag destined for the dump. The rubber muck boots were the only survivors who would live to tell the tale. It took every bit of that hour to rinse and soap, scrub, rinse, repeat (several times) to be sure that all the mud and manure had been washed away. And I still wasn't confident that the smell was gone. Hopefully the citronella candles that I'd light on the deck would mask any remaining odor. I'd finished dressing and was slicing potatoes and onions for the grill when Tommy pulled back in the driveway. He, too, was scrubbed clean and wearing fresh jeans.

He put two huge steaks on the counter and set a small cooler on the deck. "What can I do to help? And by the way, you look better."

"Thanks. Good thing you came along, except it was sort of your fault in the first place."

"Yeah, of course it was." He laughed and shook his head. "Don't get mad at me, but I don't know when I've seen anything funnier."

I laughed then, too. We pulled a couple cold beers out of the cooler and sat on the deck giggling and chatting while Tom tended the grill. I was really enjoying it, except for the fact that The Conversation was looming over us. We were going to have to get to it eventually. I tried to brush it out of my mind and just enjoy the moments as they came.

Tom flipped a steak. "Bec, where have you been? I get the feeling you're avoiding me, and you haven't been to church at all."

So much for enjoying the moment. "You're right. I have been avoiding you, and I'm sorry. I guess I've just been afraid of what happens after we have this talk."

"What?" He tilts his head. "I don't get it."

"Tom, I haven't been going to church because … well, because I just don't belong in that church. It took me awhile to figure it out, and I talked to the pastor about it."

"What do you mean, you don't belong?" He took the steaks off the grill and brought them to the table. They sizzled on the platter and Tom went back to get the bundle of potatoes. It gave me a brief moment to collect myself. He returned and sat down facing me. "Go on," he prompted.

"I was having trouble with the strict doctrine already, and then he gave this sermon about how everyone who is not of this particular faith, who is not "saved," is going to hell." Tom looked at me quizzically. "Well, that's just not what I believe."

"Um, I see. So that's why you've been avoiding me?" He cut into his steak and tasted it, gave a hum of satisfaction.

"Yes. I know how important this church is to you. And I know how serious you are about your faith. And there was also this stuff about men not being alone with women, how it's not even appropriate for a man to counsel a woman."

Tom shook his head. "Bec, that's not in the Bible, not God's law. That's a rule, or a guideline, that this church has. Each of us has to decide what fits for us."

"Do you agree with that?"

"For myself, no. But some people might need that to stay on the right path. But that's not really what we're talking about here, is it?"

"No, I guess not. It's just that I have a different take on things, spiritually I mean." I ate a couple bites of steak and potatoes. Delicious. "I believe that our souls are never separate from God, in life or in death. It's just our perception, and our ego, that allows us to think we are. I believe we're here to experience and learn the lessons we can only learn on the physical plane, and that eventually our souls return home."

Tom sat back in his chair and took a long swallow from his bottle of beer. He watched me for a minute, thinking. "That's certainly more comforting than what the Bible says about it."

I nodded. "It may be, but believe me, I didn't arrive at this because I was looking for comfort. And I'm not as well versed in the Bible as you are, but I think this is the entire point of free will."

He raised his eyebrows, his gaze intense. "What do you mean?"

"I think we are given the opportunity to face challenges here and grow spiritually, but we don't have to. Without the threat of retribution, we can freely choose to resist, because it's easier, more convenient for our egos. Or we can choose to do the work, to learn the lessons and evolve, both spiritually and as human beings."

Tommy was no longer eating. He sat quietly for several minutes, the meal forgotten. I waited for him to excuse himself and leave.

"Bec, how did you come to all this?"

"A lot of reading, a lot of searching, a lot of life, I guess. All I can tell you is that this is what I know in my heart."

"This is a discussion that we could have for hours, or years even. And we probably will. But there's really only one question I have for you."

"Okay, shoot."

"Rebecca, do you believe in God?"

"Yes, you know I do, and isn't that what I just said? We've talked about this before…."

"Exactly. And that's all I ever needed to know about you. We all find our own way."

Now it was my turn to think a moment. "You mean it doesn't matter to you if I don't go to this church?"

"Not if it doesn't matter to you that I do."

We finished our meal in leisure, sat and talked about everything and nothing until the fireflies danced and blinked around us. Tom kissed me goodnight and stepped off the deck.

"See ya later, Stinky."

CHAPTER SEVENTEEN

It's late August, and the razor edge of Jack's death has dulled, and my heart has mostly healed. Sometimes it returns in a sudden rush, and on those days there are intermittent, telltale traces of blood dripping from the open wound in my chest, but it's not unbearable or life threatening. Tommy was right—the gratitude practice helped, and I have returned to the simple flow of daily life and chores, shed the stiff, robotic motion that characterizes numbing grief.

I was truly amazed at Tom's acceptance of my flight from his church, and of our different viewpoints on the disposition of souls, both saved and unsaved. I should have been more trusting in Tom's common sense, his ability to think for himself, and there was a tremendous relief that the eventual outcome of our relationship, though still on shaky ground, was not going to be governed by the doctrine of his church.

Still, the question of where or whether we will (or will not) make our life together is a heavy burden, which I try valiantly to ignore. But it's like ignoring a prancing, pink warthog in a purple tutu. I growl at it a few times and it retreats to a dim corner, cowering.

One Saturday I had just finished mending a hole in the fence, through which Izzy had somehow squeezed her rotund, yearling body. She's a fabulous specimen of a young beefalo cow, and I can't help admiring her wide butt as I whack her with a stick, herding her back to the barn. I never did have Harry castrated, realizing right before the vet arrived with her bundle of surgical tools that he is unrelated to both Mae and Izzy, and would be a good sire for their future babies. He hasn't grown a larger brain, but so far he's remained as sweet and gentle as the day he arrived. We can charitably disregard the head butting and kicking episode in the Jeep, chalking it up to a very frightened, confused baby.

Lucy continues to stubbornly deny her Ayrshire heritage, which is normally kind and affectionate towards humans. She hates me. And she particularly hates when I touch her. Occasionally I crowd her into a corner and force her to stand to be brushed. She humps her back and squeezes her eyes shut until the torture has ended. She's smart though—the one time she swiped a sharp hoof at me and I thumped her hard on the rump, she learned the lesson and has never offered to do it again. We basically tolerate one another. I'm amused that Piglet doesn't like her much either—when he's bored, it's Lucy he singles out to push around the pasture.

I still find my peace in and around the barn, so I tend to spend a lot of time out there, puttering around, doing chores, and watching the animals graze or sleep. I'm sweeping the barn floor that Saturday when I hear someone pull in the driveway.

Tommy waves to me, grinning as usual. "C'mon, we're taking a ride."

"Where?"

"Never mind, get in the truck."

So I do. We drive in silence for the first hour. "Are we going to Vermont?"

"Yeah. Bob called and he's got some young steers to sell."

"No trailer?"

"Never a good idea to show up with a trailer when you're bargaining. He'll have to consider that, if he wants me to come back."

Halfway to the farm, Tom pulls off the highway and winds down Route 3. It takes us past the wild, tangled part of the Pemigewasset River. He stops the truck and smiles at me. "Let's go fishing."

Tommy takes two fishing rods out of the back of the truck and we walk down the steep, wooded bank to a rushing waterfall. It surges through the jumbled granite boulders and dumps into a clear, oval pool below.

"This is called Livermore Falls," I tell him. "Used to fish here in college."

"Brook trout?"

"Yup, and rainbows." I pick my way over to balance on a once-familiar rock, bait my hook, and cast. Tom watches. The first wriggling square-tail is out of the pool in a matter of minutes. He grins at me, casting his own line farther downstream.

An hour later a stringer of six good-size fish floats below us and we've stretched out on a smooth boulder to catch the last rays of the high sun. Green, fragrant moss creeps to the edge of the shade beneath the spruce trees. Tom has his hands behind his head, gazing up at the thin, white clouds.

"Now will you tell me?"

"What?"

He turns his head and looks at me, issues a warning command. "Becca …"

"I don't know, Tommy. It's not that I don't love you, God knows. But what are we supposed to do?"

His intense gaze never leaves my face. "We're supposed to get married. It's what comes next." Simple. For him.

I slide down to the edge of the stream, dangling my bare feet in the cold water. "Tom." I shake my head, trying to clear it. "Where are we supposed to live?"

"Well, I really don't care, but I can't ask Dad to move. The farm is his home, and he's eighty-years-old. It's always been his home."

"I know. But it's my home too. I mean, my house."

"No." He shakes his dark head and sets his square jaw. "Your home is with me. My home is in your heart." He hesitates, tries to find the words. "Bec, after Dad goes we can live wherever you want.

For now, it has to be the farm."

"Or not …" I'm watching the shadowy trout under the ledge across from me.

"Or not," he agrees, nodding. "But if that's what you choose … I mean, if you choose the house over us, then we have to call it quits."

"Why?"

"Because I can't live like this, and I won't."

Sweet Jesus, it's so simple for him. I feel the bile of anger rising in my throat, recognizing that it's only a masquerade party for fear. My guts cramp and ache. Do I want to lose him?

"Bec, you've been alone a long time, and so have I. Is that what scares you?"

"No." Which is a bald-faced lie of course, but it's not quite the heart of the matter.

"Then what is it?" he presses.

"What happens when you die?" I can't believe those words tumbled out of my mouth, and I look away self-consciously. It wasn't something I was even aware of thinking.

Tom stares at me, and then he laughs, huge guffaws that make me want to strangle him on the spot, leave his muscled body for the ravens and his sweet soul to find its own way home. He giggles as the tears run down his tanned cheeks.

"Well, when I die, first you get to bury me, maybe say a few words, and then you get to go back to your house."

"I'm not kidding, Tommy." Tears are dripping

off my chin and a long string of mucous is sliding down my upper lip, threatening to fall. Very pretty, I'm sure. He rolls over and wipes my face with the tail of his shirt.

"Besides, who says I die first? What if it's you that checks out, leaving me behind?"

"Tom …" I rock into the strong embrace of his chest and arms and I sob, soaking his shirt. His heart is thudding its familiar, steady rhythm under my cheek and he pats my back, smoothes my hair with his rough hand.

"It's so far away, darlin'. Do you want to waste the rest of your life, of our lives, in fear?"

"Yes," I blubber.

His bright eyes drill holes in me. "Really?"

"No. Yes. I don't know …"

"Okay. Well, you think about it. Let's get these fish in the cooler and hit the road."

Sixty miles later, as the old saying goes, the light breaks on Marblehead—Tom has asked me to marry him. What a dolt! I'm very quiet for the rest of the day, lost in a haze of wonder, seized by a scrambling panic.

Death and its crushing aftermath have followed me all my life. Not threatening me directly, but taking so many from me. The wonderful man who was *supposed* to be my mate and husband died when I was barely twenty, and he was twenty-seven. I was pregnant with his child when he died—didn't know it until two months later, but I lost the baby too. I'd never told anyone, was stone-cold silent in the shock of my immediate pain, and had finally fled from the grief, done an abrupt about face, and simply ignored it. That worked pretty well for about thirty years (until I had a complete emotional meltdown), but that defining event had a devastating impact on my ability or willingness to open myself to others whom I could have loved. Everyone was kept at a comfortable arms length, as if I could somehow avoid the inevitable cycle of life and death.

Then my grandparents died, one by one, my mother when she was barely sixty, my uncles, and my poor, lost-soul sister. Then Jack. Pretty soon I'll face another unwelcome, inevitable loss with my own elderly, failing father. For a while, they were dropping like flies and I spent a lot more time at funerals than at weddings.

The food is better at weddings.

CHAPTER EIGHTEEN

Another winter is bearing down on us, and I am wedged between a large, unwieldy rock and a financial hard place. The entire country is plunged into deep recession, and the balance in my checkbook, while never consistently robust, has deteriorated to pale and sickly. It's been an especially rainy summer, a lousy growing season, and the cost of hay has almost doubled from the year before. The faces of five hungry cows, who have grazed the once resplendent pasture down to bare, brown stubble, stare at me across the split-rail fence. Piglet has elevated the art of equine consumption to a world-class sport, though in truth, his hay needs are a mere pittance of what the cattle demand. When I tally up what the winter stores of hay to feed all six of them will be, I nearly faint. Then I make a good stiff drink.

I wander around for weeks, scheming and figuring, conjecturing about what my not-yet-earned commission checks may be in the foreseeable future. Frankly, it's not looking good. Our work in the mortgage industry has become particularly challenging. Property values have plummeted and lenders have tightened their collective belts on guidelines and loan products. Liz and I spend our days trying to pry frantic people loose from the adjustable rates they're saddled with so they can save their homes. Sometimes it works, and I don't go home crying, and sometimes it's too late already. If there is one thing we've learned, it's that our income from one month to the next is uncertain at best. It will be enough to hope that Liz and I will survive this recession ourselves.

I've also run smack up against the reality of what beef cattle are intended for: the freezer. Contrary to my dreamy delusions, they are not intended to be expensive lawn ornaments. My initial goal of raising top-quality beefalo, for both personal consumption and sale, has turned into a serious dilemma that I somehow hadn't foreseen. Once again, the specter of the slaughterhouse looms. But it's one thing to fancy oneself a farmer, to build fences, chase errant calves over hill and dale, lug grain bags, stack hundreds of hay bales, and dispose of manure by the ton—it's quite another to follow through with the killing of animals you have named, cared for, and yes, fallen in love with—even the ones that don't love you back.

At the very beginning only the imagery of peaceful, grazing cattle led me down this path—that and a possibly manic episode! If that's the case, it's worn off and now I know that I cannot afford to feed them for the winter. I certainly can't allow them to go hungry, and I can't force myself to deliver them to the grim reaper. Apples or eggplant, or even asparagus, might have been a wiser farming crop for me, though they're not very good company.

Tommy's farm is full to bursting with his multiplying herd, and he's caught in the same tight pickle I am. His own hay crop was weak and he'll have to supplement with purchased silage. Adding five more hungry mouths won't work. I'd give him the cows if he'd take them, but he would never accept them on those terms.

With one month's worth of hay remaining, I place an ad in *Uncle Henry's*, a regional classified publication. But who is going to buy cattle in October? It's a season for herd reduction, not expansion. Inexplicably, Mae has stopped bellowing. After more than a year with me, she seems to have satisfied herself that I've been sufficiently trained to deliver the goods every morning and evening. Foolish. This is further testament to the limited brain power of the bovine mind.

Two more weeks of frenzied hay inhalation tick by before the call comes. It's a beef farmer from Maine who is nearly delirious with the prospect of full-blood beefalo. He has a herd of forty-three Herefords that roam his eighty acres, and has long coveted his own dream of beefalo. He's overcome and stutters with unconcealed glee when I tell him where they came from—the Vermont farm is the pinnacle of excellence in northeast beefalo production. We talk for over an hour and agree that he will come see them the following weekend, trailer in tow.

The night before he's due, I brave a bitterly cold north wind, appropriately termed an "Arctic Clipper," and carry my dinner out to the barn. I dine with the cattle and Piglet, allowing the fog of their sweet, scented breath and the pungent, green aroma of their manure to bathe me in warm, humid waves as I eat, trying to swallow around the lump in my throat. The same country radio station is playing—it's been interrupted only by the occasional power outage. This is how it began, and this is how it will end.

Some farmers are rough around the edges, silent to the point of surliness. This is not the case with Paul. He arrives with a farmer friend, chattering like a gregarious blue jay, almost giggling with enthusiasm as he shakes my hand. He can hardly wait to see the cattle in question. I've contained everyone in the barn and they are milling restlessly as we enter. Mae raises her head and eyes the stranger suspiciously, places her enormous body between him and the others. Jackie peeks around at him under Mae's tail.

Though he tries to follow the accepted, close-mouthed method of livestock surveying, giving little away, I can see it in his bright eyes. He's in love. I'm trying to maintain the stiff upper lip expected of New Englanders, so we almost ignore one another as he watches them. His friend is getting antsy—they have a long drive home.

"What about the Ayrshire?" Paul finally asks.

"I don't know." I shrug and turn to him. "She's a freemartin, basically useless, so I guess I'll keep her. But I'm worried that the horse is going to pick on her if she's alone."

He eyes Piglet with distaste. "Ayuh. Wouldn't have a horse on my place. She'll be wicked lonely by herself."

"I know. Maybe I should keep Harry, or Jackie." I point at the bull and the little heifer.

"No! I gotta have 'em all. He's gonna be my herd bull, and I need the girls for foundation stock." He nods at Lucy. "I'll take her, too. My daughter's got a fondness for dairy cows. She's awful damn pretty with that dark red coat. Not having to milk her is a plus, far as I'm concerned."

"But will you kill her?"

"Lady, I got an eighteen-year-old Hereford who hasn't had a calf in years. Can't bring myself to put her down. Wife thinks I'm nuts. You sell me that bull and I'll promise her a home forever."

Paul meets my price without a squabble. It's more than enough to cover Piglet's hay for the winter. This all sounds like the perfect solution, until my plump, hide-covered kids are herded onto the stock trailer and the gate is closed. Harry was by far the hardest, my sweet bottle-fed orphan who still trots to me for a good head scratch, and swipes his rough tongue over my hands. I cling to the back of the trailer, and he looks up at me through the metal slats, offers a soft, lowing moo of concern. I love him, and he loves me. The tears stream down my cheeks and Paul glances away and lights a cigarette, the moment beyond awkward for him. I doubt he's ever had this particular experience at the auction yards: a lamenting seller, sniffling and blubbering over a successful sale. He pats my shoulder and clears his throat.

"Don't worry, dear. They'll live a long, happy life at my place. Come visit them anytime you want."

His friend laughs and slaps his knee. "Were you two separated at birth or somethin'? Never saw two people who love cows so damn much."

I may be a simpleton, or desperate for their assurance, but I believe them both.

The first night was difficult. Okay, it was horrible. Piglet wandered the dark pasture, his hoof beats thudding across the frost-hardened ground, calling for them intermittently. I lay in bed listening to him walk and whinny, achingly aware of the long silences in between. In the morning we're both bleary-eyed. Piglet stands at the hay pile, looking around for someone, anyone, to push around. He whinnies once more, then settles to his lonely breakfast.

At the diner, Tommy joins me at the counter. "Did he show up?"

"Uh huh. They're gone—all of them."

He stares straight ahead. "For the best, my dear. Plenty of calves coming in the spring. You can borrow a couple for summer pasture if you want."

This is precisely the soothing balm I need. He could not have offered anything better in that moment.

CHAPTER NINETEEN

Red Gate Farm has morphed into something beyond a livestock feeding station. It has a new purpose in life, and so do I. One fall morning when the cows were still in residence, and I was shoveling the fourteenth or fifteenth ton of manure out of the barn, I got to wondering why I'd named it "Red Gate" in the first place. It had just come to me, but why? What significance did this particular name hold for me? No sooner had I posed this question than the answer suddenly materialized in my brain: Red Gate = Heart. This little farm is the gateway to my heart, the inner realm. Hmmph. Interesting. But it didn't answer the question.

Why name it at all when there was no one here but me? Why go to the trouble of sinking the fence post, building the gate, and painting it? I certainly wasn't selling anything of value, didn't need to draw the general public into my little private domain. Was I simply advertising to my neighbors, and all passersby for that matter, that I did indeed have a heart?

Was it a lonely heart? Or a heart overflowing with love for my fellow man? A breaking heart? Maybe a seeking heart. Bingo! And what had I been seeking all these years, months, days? I pondered this in waking and sleeping hours. I watched Piglet graze and I wondered. The thing that kept coming to me was not comforting in the least. Grief and loss, and the occasional persistent depression, had walked with me for years. Exactly what was I trying to say here, or trying to unconsciously create?

When I asked *that* question, the thing that formed in my mind was just the tiniest bit unsettling. No, in truth, it was startling. It had begun with the broken fawn and the orphaned calf. It had begun when I invited Jack to die in my home.

I'm not sure you'll take this leap with me, because it doesn't follow a conscious, clear, or straight path. But suddenly, I knew. What I wanted to create was a safe, healing haven for others who were silently grieving, who were facing loss so staggering that they could not find the words to describe it, nor the will and desire to survive it.

I'd been there. For thirty years I'd been in that place, unable to speak about the devastation in my wounded heart, unwilling to confront it and move through it. That resistance and silence had kept me single and separate for most of my adult life. Though I loved her desperately, the irrational fear of losing my sweet, beautiful daughter had made me keep a reserved distance from even her. It had taken a complete mental and emotional breakdown for me to finally speak my own truth in this. I'd lost my career over it, and nearly lost my own life. Since then I'd been flubbing around in the financial arena. I liked it—it was okay (when we were making a living). But it wasn't soul satisfying. There were too many people in desperate circumstances that we couldn't help, and they weighed heavy on me.

So I found myself at this unexpected crossroads, with perhaps twenty or thirty years left on this earth—what was I going to do with that time? I wasn't sure exactly how I was going to accomplish it, or exactly what it would look like when it was done, but I knew that I would offer my farm as a retreat for others who were suffering their own losses, their own private, isolated grief. Here at Red Gate they would find refuge and solace. If I did it well enough, they would begin to find their own peace.

It's not an easy business plan to write, so esoteric in its nature, and even more challenging to sell to hard-nosed commercial lenders. There was a lot to do, and I needed more funds than languished in my meager farm account to accomplish it. But just as I was preparing myself for a long, tedious battle of begging and pleading, the right lender appeared.

At our first meeting, three middle-aged business men in dark suits sat at a conference table, blank legal pads before them, pens poised for note taking. They listened thoughtfully as I outlined the concept, then asked a few pointed questions about target markets.

"Has anyone in this room *not* lost a loved one?" I asked. No one moved. "All right then, we can agree that this is an inevitable part of life—virtually no one escapes this." They nodded.

"Is there anyone you can think of who has struggled with a loved one's death, someone who couldn't find their peace with it? Or perhaps someone who became overwhelmed with grief, completely withdrawing from their normal life, and from everyone who loves them?"

Two of the men nod slowly, and one looks away, staring out the window at the far end of the room. He's reluctant to turn back, and when he does, there are tears in his eyes.

"It doesn't have to be that way. They don't have to suffer like that. There are abundant resources, but by their very nature, grief and depression usually prevent people from reaching out. There is a profound lethargy in the midst of all the pain. If they do try to speak about it, others often try to soothe and comfort them, or offer well-worn, empty platitudes."

One of the men clears his throat. "What are you proposing then?"

"I'm suggesting that rather than allow this paralyzed state of grief to go on indefinitely, rather than watch people suffer with this for months or years on end, that they retreat to a place where they can talk and grieve and heal together."

"Do you mean a sort of 'grief rehab'?"

"No. Believe me, discarding the pain cold turkey, as if it were an alcohol or drug addiction, is not the answer. The only way out of the pain is through it. But they can be supported and encouraged through the process, without the demands and distractions of regular life for a little while."

"And how would you go about finding these people?" He's leaning forward, intent and interested, but doubtful.

This question stops me. I'm not sure how to find them, or if they will even come once I do. "I don't know. I think they'll find me." It's a leap of faith and the best I can do.

Two weeks later I get their answer: they are taking this leap with me, and they're backing it with real money! The next few months are a whirlwind of activity on my little farm. Tommy's borrowed calves and Piglet watch the carpenters and machinery that move around the place from dawn to dusk, building, landscaping, tearing down, resurrecting. Tug trots back and forth, supervising and amusing the men. Finally, it is complete.

New, lush gardens are tucked into sunny corners, and stone paths wind past them, offering benches on which to rest and reflect. The derelict, antique barn has been stripped to its huge, timber bones, new sills replace the rotten ones, and it is dressed in bright pine planks that were cut and milled on Tom's farm. The interior is redesigned into a central meeting hall, a commercial kitchen, six separate bedrooms and three shared bathrooms. Even before it's furnished and decorated, it glows with warm light, breathes with a peaceful energy. It's more than I expected, more than I ever dreamt it would be.

I've interviewed and lined up grief counselors, healers, Reiki masters and massage therapists, a talented chef and support staff. Everything is in place. Now the only question remaining is whether Red Gate will ever see its first guest. There's been some interest, but no confirmed reservations. I'm standing under a shade tree when the general contractor comes to hand me his final bill.

"Uh, I think it's great what you're doing here." He wipes his dirty palms on his dirtier jeans, scuffs his booted feet in the fresh gravel of the driveway.

"Thanks, John. I really appreciate your help. Your men did a great job."

He nods, surveys the finished project. "You know, my daughter's having a tough time right now. Her two best friends died in a car accident—she was supposed to be with them." He chokes up and stops, shaking his head.

"That must be very difficult for her. When did this happen, John?"

"Almost a year ago, but she's not getting over it, just getting worse, far as I can tell. I think she feels guilty."

"She should talk to someone, you know."

"Well, that's what I'm getting at. Do you think she could come here? I'll trade that last bill for it."

"John! Your daughter is welcome, but that's too much money. I'll get you a fee schedule and brochure. Wait here."

He reaches out one meaty paw, stops me from going. "Don't need it. If you can help her, it's a small price to pay. Besides, most of it's padded." He grins and walks to his truck. "I'll have her call you. Her name is Cynthia."

I take this as a very favorable omen. My mother's name was Cynthia.

CHAPTER TWENTY

Red Gate's first year was not a smashing financial success, but it survived. What's more important is that the majority of people who came, morose and withdrawn when they arrived, left with lighter hearts, smiling and grateful. If not transformed, they were at least well on the way through their own journey, and they'd found the voice to share it with others. At the very least, they were no longer isolated. I learned so much from each of them, and it was not always a comfortable process.

As with so many born and bred Yankees, my family had prided themselves on building and defining their character through hard work, self-reliance, and stoicism. Each generation had absorbed the lesson and passed it on successfully: The intrusion of pain, a human condition as inevitable and natural as the sun rising every morning, was a clear signal to retreat, to handle it on your own. When you'd moved through it (or buried it) and were fit for human company, you could rejoin the fold.

So this thing I'd created was as foreign a way of life to me as it was to most of my guests. One thing it taught me was that cows are not the best company. They serve a purpose, of course, and I'm still helplessly in love with them. They are serene and peaceful, and just watching them fills me with a calm contentment. Some people like a tropical fish tank. I like cows. But cows alone are not enough.

Moving forward in my own journey of the heart takes longer than I'd like to admit, and seasons pass, marked by the particular chores that they bring. Eventually I warm to it—not with an abundance of grace, not without conflict or stubborn resistance. Tom had delivered the summer calves as promised, and then he began his own final retreat. Suddenly I understand that my life will be remarkably diminished and dramatically off course without him. I understand finally that we were brought together, as help mates, as soul mates. I'm half without him, a concept that had always irritated me. Are we not whole unto ourselves? And the answer is this: *No.* We are not.

Like it or lump it, we are part of a community of human beings, part and parcel of the universe that surrounds us, part of God's creation. And He did not create us to be lost, alone and adrift. This is much easier for me to understand in concept than gracefully embrace in practice. My ingrained thirty-year habit of isolation and self-preservation had allowed ego to run rampant, allowed me to define myself as separate from everyone else, different and distinct. Finally, with the stunning example of the people who have allowed me to help them, I relinquish this arrogant position, lay down the paralyzing fright and step away from it. Step towards Tom and his welcoming, patient heart.

Our wedding is the strangest, loveliest thing I've ever seen. There are only twenty of us, and we spread out on the lawn beside the house. My house. My father stands beside Earl, grins at me, tears shining in his old blue eyes as he watches me pledge the rest of my life to this man he barely knows. But it's easy to know Tom. He is just exactly what he seems.

Tommy's pastor is beaming as he leads us through the simple, short ceremony. Though I only attend service there on rare occasion, he continues to offer caring counsel and trusted friendship to both of us. He likes weddings, adores it when the people he loves make the commitment to love, honor, and cherish one another. Tom beams, too. He wraps his arms around my waist and pulls me tight to him.

The food is wonderful. Earl has grilled ducks and geese, thick beefalo steaks and great slabs of meaty ribs. Tom has made baked beans and fluffy biscuits, and his sisters have roasted garden vegetables and made pies enough to feed a hundred people. My contribution is a platter of plump deviled eggs—I think that's funny and Tommy shakes his head, laughing.

"Thank you, darlin'. I'm a happy man."

"You're a goof ball," I tell him.

He nods. "You understand you belong to me now?"

"Tommy, you and I have always belonged to each other. It just took us thirty years to find one another."

His black eyebrows arch high. "Really? So this was your plan all along?"

"Something like that. And what about you? Do you belong to me now?"

"It's my job to take care of you, Rebecca."

"But do you *belong* to me?"

"In a way you wouldn't understand. It's different for men."

"How is it different?"

"I would give my life to protect and keep you." His voice is low and fierce, growling out of his thick, sun-burned throat. It staggers me with the force of his emotion. There is nothing else to say and we join our guests.

After the meal has been cleared away, Tom's sisters and I leave the men and we drive down to the lake, sit in the sun-warmed sand, talking and laughing.

"What's going on?" I ask. "What are they doing?"

"Tommy has a surprise for you, and we've got strict orders not to take you back to the farm till dark."

"Oh." What is he up to? I wonder if he's got more cows to show off, present me with a wedding gift of cattle. "Cows?" I ask, frowning.

Kate nearly passes out, she laughs so hard. The others smile and shake their heads, giggling into their hands.

"C'mon, tell me."

"We can't—we promised." They all nod in unison.

Finally it's time. The sun is setting over the lake, behind the dusky, blue-green of the surrounding mountains. We get in the car and drive the few short miles to the farm. Candles glow in the windows. The girls snicker and leave me at the front steps. Tommy stands in the kitchen doorway, leaning against it.

"You coming in?" I walk up the granite stairs and he takes my hand. "Welcome home," he whispers, kissing me full and hard, making me melt into him.

I've never spent one night in this strange, rambling house. "Tom …"

"Shhh. Come with me." He leads me through the utilitarian kitchen and into the living room. I think he's taking me to the bedroom, but he stops.

"Where's your father?"

"He's over at Kate's for the night." I look up at him and he's grinning. "See anything different?"

I turn slowly and there they are. All around me are my grandmother's antiques, and the small items that I cherish, simply because I've lived with them for fifty-five years. They identify people and pieces of my past, and are part of the intricate fabric of my solitary life that I wasn't sure I wanted to relinquish to be with him.

"Tommy …" I can't really speak and my throat is constricted with a gigantic lump that threatens to explode. He looks very pleased with himself. He overflows with pride and love, and his eyes glitter in the candlelight.

"Tom, you didn't have to do this."

"I figured you'd given up enough for me. It's the only thing I could think of."

"What about Earl? This was okay with him?"

"Loved it. Loves you."

I've wandered over to run my hand over the polished, two-hundred year old pine sideboard that began its beautiful, useful life in Ireland. "Why didn't you tell me about this?"

"Because you needed to come to me on your own. I didn't want to bribe you." I start to choke up and tears threaten to spill over. He steps close, lifts my chin. "Our wedding day isn't one for tears, even happy tears." But his eyes are shimmering too.

"How did you know that this would help?"

"Pastor told me. He said women's things help them out during change." He smiles softly, shyly. "Was he right?"

"Yes."

"How come?" He truly doesn't understand.

"Because, Tom … because it makes it my home too."

"Well, I thought I did that."

"More than you will ever know," I tell him.

He kisses me long and deeply. "Well then,

woman, get in the bedroom and behave like a good wife should!" He smacks my butt and I wiggle away from him, laughing.

"You thought you were getting a good wife in this bargain?" He howls, pushes me ahead of him into the bedroom. My polished brass bed gleams in the candlelight.

"The bed, too?"

"Yup. Just in case. Just for good measure."

CHAPTER TWENTY-ONE

Red Gate Farm continues to operate, gaining momentum every season. It's only four miles from Tommy's farm and I spend part of every day there visiting with the guests, going over the books, and talking with the management team. A property caretaker has moved into my house, and besides his many chores, he tends the few cows that Tom leaves there for summer pasture, and for the guests to enjoy. Many of them do, and the cows have learned that oatmeal cookies are often handed out across the fence. For those that are not besotted by bovines, there are hundreds of wild birds visiting the stocked feeders, and the requisite tropical fish tank in the center's Great Room.

I love Red Gate, but it is no longer my home. Tom was right—my home is with him.

We've slaughtered the latest crop of Tom's beefalo herd, and the freezers are packed full with dark-red steaks, roasts, stew meat, and hamburger. Not Harry's first born son who I'd purchased from Farmer Paul. The spitting image of his sire, Henry follows me around like a big, dumb dog. I told Tom before we married that Henry would die of nothing short of doddering old age on the farm. He nodded, accepting without question or comment, and it will be Harry's grandchildren that will buck and frolic in the pasture in the springs to come. But I wasn't looking forward to that first day, was dreading the sight of the newly killed, naked bodies hanging from the barn rafters, their names crossed off the herd book.

Fortunately, I was spared, even if they were not. Tom never asked. He sent me off with a list of chores that I could not possibly accomplish in one short, fall day, but it kept me off the farm from dawn to dark. When I returned, it was over, and except for the lingering, coppery scent of blood, no outward trace remained in the barn yard. He built a walk-in cooler during the summer and the beef sides were hanging in there to age. Unless I ventured beyond its stainless steel door, I would never have to see. I was grateful for that consideration. I loved him all the more for it. Tom made dinner that night. We had roast chicken and fresh green beans.

I'll never be able to say this right, but here goes. "Husband and wife" in your fifties is remarkably different than in your twenties. First, nothing looks the same. No amount of physical labor is going to retrieve the hard, slim bodies that youth graced us with. But it's a partnership that isn't possible when you're young and wild, driven by jumbled hormones and biological clocks, confused and caught in self-indulgent ego. It isn't grandly exciting, or nervy and edgy, and there is a distinct lack of shared history from the previous thirty years. There is no possibility of raising a family, and yet, you have become one. But no one is struggling to find their way in life or love. Not to say there are not the occasional challenges, but they're softer and gentler, infinitely more tolerant of the differences, boundlessly more grateful for the small things. In disagreements, no one panics, nor comes away bloodied and bruised.

Earl passed away last winter, quietly in his sleep one night and surrounded by his family. Tommy cried and his sisters wept, but they knew how to comfort one another. They knew how to accept comfort from others. And then they lifted their chins and squared their shoulders, leaning back into the work. I learned a lot through all of it. The chores of the farm and the gentle rhythm of the passing seasons soothed the raw, hurt places.

Cattle bellowed for their hay, and steaming, wet calves bawled as they were born. In the spring, corn and squash began their journey towards the sun. In the summer, dragonflies snapped bugs out of the cobalt sky and the hay crop was baled, minus one pair of helping hands. That fall we had a harvest feast, invited our friends, family, and neighbors to join us at the farm. Our farm.

Tom gave me the choice then. "Do you want to go home?"

"This is our home."

He nods and turns me to face him. "Bec, I know. But I promised you we could go back if you wanted."

"No, Tom. This is our home."

I washed the dishes from supper, and filled the woodstove while he fiddled with an old chainsaw on the porch. Tug curled at his feet. Ungrateful mutt. Always had been my dog, but he'd long since ditched me for my handsome husband.

"Tommy, I'm going to bed now. You coming?"

"In a minute, sweetheart."

Seriously. Sweetheart? When did that happen? "Okay, pumpkin …"

He points at me with a rasp. "Don't start without me."

"Really? Or what?"

Tom leans back on the porch post. He grins and my heart is warmed all over again, for the hundredth time that day. He's done countless tiny things, as he does every day, to let me know that I am loved. So far he has taken his wedding vows very seriously, and he's better at it than me. I still have the occasional fit of pride and ego, but it seems they are beginning to diminish in frequency the longer I live with this generous man.

Standing in the light from the kitchen doorway, I take my flannel shirt off, twirling it in my fingers. He raises his eyebrows, pretending shock.

"A sin?" I ask.

"Not even close."

"How about this?" I run my palm over the cool flesh of my breasts and his eyes widen. "Or this?" My hand skinnies inside the waistband of my denim skirt.

"Geez, Bec, could you just let me finish with the saw?"

"Sure. Your choice."

I smile at him and wander back into the house. I hear him set the saw on the bench outside the door, and I race through the empty house towards the bedroom. He catches up to me in the living room and drags me down to the floor. His eyes are shining and his lips are twitching with playful mischief. I kiss him till the breath huffs from his broad, muscled chest. The raging bull tattoo ripples under my hand.

"You are nothin' but trouble," he mutters.

"Uh huh. Are you going to behave like a good husband should?"

"What have you gotten me into?"

"Love."

"Ummmm." He quiets, moving over me with a gentle, intense rhythm that I've come to know so well. A host of angels delivers him unto me. God knew what he was doing when he created this. God knew exactly what he was doing when he brought us together.

The rest was up to me and Tom.

The End

AUTHOR'S NOTE

This manuscript turned out to be much more than the simple recording of an emerging lifestyle on my small farm, and the emergence of childhood dreams into reality. And it was more than the fanciful fiction of a sweet love story, which is what it really wanted to grow up to be.

It actually began as nothing more than a photo journal of the injured fawn, and I thought that it might make a good article or short story for a local paper, maybe even a regional magazine. Then Harry came, and somewhere along the line, I discovered that I was perilously close to falling in love with my farmer friend. Though I've been round the block more than a few times, know the inherent dangers in getting carried away with what might turn out to be nothing more than a brief infatuation, somehow I knew that the feelings I had for him, and the desires that I was holding for him, were right on target. I had rarely felt so certain about anything in my life. That didn't mean it was going to work out—I know better than that.

So I decided to write my way into what I hoped would become an eventual reality. I often use this technique to work through my thoughts and feelings for what's in my direct and obvious path of experience. I'm not in the habit of publishing these playful meanderings—they are useful tools for me personally, sort of a pre-game warm up. And it's always fun to see how close I can come.

This time it was different. This time I was literally attempting to manifest the future by creating it in the present, on paper.

A week after sending the first draft to my publisher for review, another book came into my hands: Jerry and Esther Hicks *Ask & It Is Given*, the latest in their remarkable books that are co-written with the non-physical entity, Abraham. I'd never read any of their previous works, so it was a new experience, and much to my surprise, its subject was exactly what I had just done: *How to manifest your future reality by creating it in thought and intention in the present, holding it in loving, prayerful gratitude as if it had already arrived.*

Could have knocked me over with a feather, but it gave me confidence that I was on the right path. Now, according to Abraham, I would just have to hold that dream in my heart and wait for it to unfold. I would simply have to allow it to manifest in the physical realm. Nothing more. Trust God, the Angels, and the Universe to bring it forth through the open channel of my clear intention.

Sounds simple enough, but I'm the sort of person who likes to help these things along a bit ... okay, alright, I like to force outcomes. This time I promised myself that I would sit back and wait, and trust that all was well. Sure, I tripped and faltered, fell flat on my face a few times, made silly awkward advances in my own interest, and from my old nemesis—impatience. But mostly I waited.

My publisher loved the manuscript and because she had read a previous non-fiction work of mine, suggested that I should wait to live the rest of it, rather than write it first. It took me awhile to convince her that it already was reality, albeit perhaps an invisible, parallel one that would never actually reveal itself. It is much to her credit that she accepted that and plunged in. And the publishing world moves so slowly that by the time we were ready for release, the story had unfurled its own version of reality. Was it the same?

No, of course not. Because something far greater, more intelligent and loving than we can possibly comprehend has its own agenda. Though we are responsible for our own lives, we are not the sole creator of them. However, it is a universal law that we must live with the consequences, joys, and sorrows of what we choose from the options that are laid before us. Each of them is a blessing, an opportunity for personal and spiritual growth, even when the process hurts (and it usually does).

You are holding in your hands, and have hopefully enjoyed, an account of my *imagined* life in this process of creation. Some of it was dead on, and some of it never actually happened. But it might! I played with time like modeling clay, and used poetic license shamelessly to alter some events that did occur. I will leave it to you to take what you like from it.

The people are all real, though most of their names have been changed. "Tom" is real, and I asked his permission to use him as my male character model. He was very gracious, flattered even, and I sincerely hope he won't regret it. The animals are all real, and I didn't feel it was necessary to change their names. By God's good grace and love, and the magnificent abundance of the Universe, I have been truly blessed to know each and every one of them.

I now hold the hope and intention that *your* dreams come true. I really do.

[illegible]

[illegible] - [illegible]